DEATH AND THE SKY ABOVE

Life held very little for Louise Hilary: drunken, bitter, vicious, and middle-aged, she was soon to leave it. Husband Charles Hilary, who had become appalled at the change in Louise over the years, found himself accused of his wife's murder, then tried, convicted, and sentenced to hang.

A few hours before the execution comes a development surprising as a bombshell . . .

DEATH AND THE SKY ABOVE

Andrew Garve

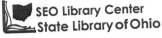

First published 1953
by
William Collins Sons & Co. Ltd

This edition 2004 by BBC Audiobooks Ltd
published by arrangement with
the author's estate

ISBN 0 7540 8659 3

British Library Cataloguing in Publication Data available

Printed and bound in Great Britain by
Antony Rowe Ltd., Chippenham, Wiltshire

Part One

CHAPTER I

IT was half past nine in the morning when the ringing of her bedside telephone roused Louise Hilary from her doped sleep. She resisted the summons as long as she could; then, as the ringing went on, she groped for the ivory receiver and dragged it on to her pillow.

"Who is it?" she mumbled.

"Hallo, Louise. It's Charles."

"Oh!" There was a hostile pause. "What do *you* want?"

"Haven't you read my letter?"

"What letter?"

"I posted it last night—you must have it by now."

"Well, I haven't. It's probably on the mat."

"Then please get it and read it. Louise, I've got to see you. Can I call this afternoon?"

Her face puckered as she tried to remember what day of the week it was. Thursday?—no, Friday. "It's no good," she said. "I'm going away today—I'll be packing this afternoon."

"Then I shall have to come this morning. It's absolutely vital that I see you. How about twelve noon?"

"Oh, all right—if you must." She dropped the receiver back on its rest, mentally cursing her husband.

Pushing aside the rumpled sheets she emerged naked from the bed and thirstily gulped water from a large tumbler. She always felt dehydrated in the mornings.

She picked up a flimsy silk dressing-gown from the floor and stood for a moment gazing at herself in the long mirror. Her face, smudged with yesterday's make-up, was a ruin. Her eyes were bloodshot at the corners, her cheeks gaunt. She could feel a tremor in her tongue, and her hands were shaky. I'm becoming a hag, she thought. Every day a little worse. But at least her figure was all right—a bit on

5

the thin side, perhaps, but pretty good for a woman of forty. Her breasts were as firm as a girl's. As long as men still liked her body, she told herself cynically, she could get by with her face. And they certainly did—too much sometimes.

She frowned as she thought of Max Raczinsky, with his stupid demands and threats. What a bore these jealous types were! It wasn't even as though he had any right to be possessive—he had absolutely nothing to offer, apart from a strong young body and a rather good technique. No money to speak of, no car except a ramshackle old two-seater, not even a flat of his own. No comfort at all. And really, she couldn't be blamed for getting fed up with those risky and unsatisfactory hotel week-ends. Now with Gerald it was going to be quite a different matter—a substantial income and a convenient apartment in a big impersonal block made an ideal combination. They'd be able to have lots of fun when he got back from Canada. Meanwhile, the sooner she left London the better—she hadn't liked that look in Max's eyes at all. Probably he hadn't meant what he'd said, but you could never be sure with Poles. She must remember to ring up about her ticket.

She wrapped the dressing-gown round her and pushed her feet into mules and went down to get the letter. Charles had been so pressing that she felt some curiosity about its contents. But when she spread the four closely-written sheets out on her pillow, sprawling full length with a cigarette smouldering between her lips, she found that it was the same old story. The only new thing was a note of desperation which was very satisfying. He was obviously in a pretty bad state, or he'd never have courted the humiliation of another meeting with her after what had happened before. "My last appeal to you ...!" She smiled sourly. Not it! He'd go on asking—what else could he do? And she'd go on refusing. The thought of his impending visit gave her vindictive pleasure.

Her head still felt as though it were filled with damp blotting-paper and she took a benzedrine tablet to wake herself up. That was routine, like the luminal at night. She ran a bath and lay in it for twenty minutes, the warm water soothing her inflamed nerves. Then she went down to the kitchen, still in dressing-gown and mules, and made

6

coffee. She drank it strong, glancing through the news-paper and chain-smoking. She ate nothing—she was never hungry in the mornings.

Back in her room she settled herself at the dressing-table for the daily rites. The hennaed hair, cut short and curled all over her head to hide its scantiness, presented no prob-lem. But the face had to be worked on. Plenty of thick foundation to hide the coarsened skin; rouge placed high to divert attention from the long down-curving lines that gave her that haggard look. Bright lipstick, plastered on; black eyebrow lines painted as thin as her shaking hand would allow, and more than a touch of mascara. The eyes them-selves would brighten under the influence of benzedrine and she would still pass as a striking woman, except with the more discerning. But the men who fell for her were the less discerning, and they liked plenty of make-up.

Before dressing, she made a perfunctory attempt to clear up some of the previous day's disorder. It was a luxurious maisonette that Charles had provided for her, and expen-sively furnished, but she never bothered about keeping it decent. She had always regarded it as a bribe that hadn't come off, and the sight of it looking tatty didn't worry her. In a perverse sort of way, it even pleased her. She gathered the cushions from the floor in the sitting-room, scraping at a bit of burnt carpet with her nail; emptied the lipsticked butts from the brimming ash-tray, and removed a wet glass from the polished top of the new television set. The smell of last night's dregs was enough to set her off. Crossing to the bottle of Trinidad rum on the tray, she poured out a third of a tumbler, added a splash of ginger-ale, and took a long drink. Her day had begun.

Charles Hilary parked his car on the leafy side of the Kensington street, out of the blazing June sun, and ap-proached the mews with a long, purposeful stride. He was a tall, slim man, bare-headed and youthful-looking, with a lean thoughtful face permanently tanned by twenty years in the sub-tropics. Though the door of No. 1 had been left open for him he knocked as any stranger would have done and waited for his wife's invitation before entering.

Apart from a momentary glimpse he had had of her one lunch-time in Piccadilly, when she had been getting into a taxi with a man, he hadn't set eyes on her for nearly five months, and the shock of her appearance stopped him on the threshold of the sitting-room like a blow. He had been prepared for some deterioration, for he could guess only too well the sort of life she was leading, but this mask of a face would have been grotesque in a professional street-walker. Affection had long since died in him, but the memory of the pretty and vivacious girl he had married still lingered on, and he felt appalled at the change in her. For a moment he forgot what she was doing to his life, and gazed at her in pity.

"When you've finished staring . . .!" she said irritably. She didn't trouble to move. She was lounging on the settee in a well-cut but crumpled black suit, with a magazine on her lap and an empty tumbler beside her. The air was heavy with perfume and the sickly smell of rum.

"I'm sorry. How are you, Louise?"

"As though you cared!" She put the magazine aside and shot him a glance of pure hatred. As always, every-thing about him jarred on her—his good looks, his quiet manner, his healthy out-of-doors appearance, his pretended concern for her. But today, she observed with satisfac-tion, there was more than a hint of strain about him, of nerves near breaking point.

"Have a drink," she said. "You're going to need it."

"Not just now, thanks."

"Well, get me one."

"Look, Louise," he said, ignoring her demand, "I want to talk to you seriously."

"You always did."

"This is the last time, I promise you."

She shrugged. "No drink, no talk. Please yourself."

He sighed, and turned to the tray. "What is it—the usual?"

"The usual." Louise smiled maliciously. "Remember introducing me to it in Port-of-Spain? 'A pretty good drink,' you said."

"I couldn't know you were going to make it your boon companion." Charles picked up the bottle of rum, poured out two fingers of the pale amber liquid, added a little ginger-ale, and passed the glass to her. Louise took it and drank and set it down.

8

"Well?" she said.

"By now you've read my letter, I hope?"

"I've glanced through it."

Charles controlled himself with difficulty. He'd known all along that he was probably wasting his time, but in this letter he had sacrified both pride and reticence in a supreme effort to reach her heart, and indifference was the hardest thing of all to take. Still, losing his temper wouldn't help.

"Did you gather enough of the contents to form a view about it," he asked, "or must I go over the ground again?"

"If you want to grovel, grovel by all means, but it won't make a scrap of difference. I shall never divorce you—you can make up your mind to that. You'll be my husband till death us do part!"

The gloating finality of her tone shocked him. She had always said she wouldn't divorce him, but this malevolent glee was something new. If she felt like that about it, there really seemed no point in going on. Half-heartedly, he played the only card that might have value.

"You'd be better off financially."

"I do quite nicely, thanks." She got up and recharged her glass and sat down again. "You couldn't buy a divorce from me if you were Rockefeller."

"You may not continue to do nicely if there's no divorce. I could stop your allowance."

"Nonsense! I'd sue you."

"No court would give you a thousand a year tax-free. Have some sense, Louise. It's far more than my income at the moment, and if it weren't for the legacy I couldn't do it." He glanced round the room. "You wouldn't be able to live like this on a court order, you know."

"And you wouldn't let it go to court—you're much too sensitive a plant. You'd hate the nasty publicity, wouldn't you? Anyway, you're not the only man in the world. I'd get by—don't worry."

"Aren't you taking rather a chance? As you say, there are other men. I may be able to divorce *you*, in time. Then where would you be?"

"You'd have to find the men first."

"I don't suppose that would be difficult."

"That's just where you're wrong. Of course, I know you're far too fastidious to employ horrid little detectives to

9

watch people, but all the same I don't believe in taking risks. I'm very discreet. It's a nuisance sometimes, having to be so careful, but it's worth it. No, you'll never free yourself that way."

He looked at her, baffled. "Louise," he said, "I wish I could understand your attitude. It isn't as though you care for me yourself . . ."

"Care for you? I loathe the sight of you."

"Then you're keeping us tied together out of sheer spite?"

"How right you are! A bitch in the manger. That's the way it is, and that's the way it's going to be."

"I can't think why you should hate me so."

"Can't you? I've told you enough times, heaven knows. I hate you for ruining my life—for taking me out to those filthy islands and leaving me to rot while you went off on your idiotic work. That's why."

"You could have come with me—you knew I wanted you to."

"To camp in the bush and study the cocoa virus? Thanks a lot."

"Other women managed to be happy out there."

"I'm not other women. You should have seen what was happening and done something about it before it was too late. You're to blame for what I've become, and I'll never forgive you for it, never!"

Charles sat staring at the floor. The gap between them was too wide to be bridged. He knew it was useless to speak, but his sense of justice revolted all the same.

I told you what it would be like, he wanted to say, *I told you the Caribbean was squalid as well as lovely, I told you it would be hot, and that some women wilted out there. I told you I should be away in the bush for pretty long spells and that if you didn't come with me you'd be lonely. I told you the work fascinated me, and that I wasn't ambitious, and that being the wife of a Director of Agriculture wouldn't be like being a Governor's lady. I told you all that before we left. I didn't know you had your own romantic ideas and were scarcely even listening—I thought you understood. I didn't know that you'd hate the life and that you wouldn't be able to get on with the coloured people. I didn't know that you'd resent my work and despise me for wanting to help them.*

I didn't know that you hadn't any inner resources and that you couldn't bear the least discomfort. I didn't know that you'd refuse to have children because you were afraid of spoiling your figure, and that you'd prefer playing bridge and talking scandal to any job of work. I didn't know that you'd let rum get hold of you so that you couldn't live without it. I didn't know, God help me, that you were just a pretty, shallow, worthless woman. I was in love with you and I took you out too soon, before I really knew you, because my leave was almost over and I couldn't bear that we should part—and perhaps that was wrong of me. But to say that I'm responsible for the wreck you've become . . .!

That was how he wanted to defend himself, but re-criminations seemed pointless now, and anyhow the grain of truth in her accusation kept him silent.

"All right," he said at last, in as matter-of-fact a voice as he could manage, "you loathe me. I never realised quite how much, but I do now. You want to punish me for what you think I've done to you. But, Louise, I'm not the only one involved. There's Kathryn. She's done you no harm—she's taken nothing you wanted. Can't you be generous to her?"

"Why should I? I *hate* her."

He stared at her in astonishment. "How can you say that? You've never met her—you've never even seen her."

"Oh, yes, I have." She glanced across at the television set. "I've watched her—often. I could kill her."

He followed the direction of her gaze, and suddenly he understood what it was that had warped her mind and filled her heart with such bitter and implacable hatred. He had a mental picture of the room in darkness and the screen lit up and Louise sitting alone in a haze of rum and self-pity, a physical and moral wreck, watching the other woman who was young, and vital, and charming, and happy as she herself would never be again. "Look here, upon this picture, and on this . . ." Knowing herself inferior in all respects but one—power—power to harm!

"Yes, I see," he said slowly. "That's—pretty horrible."

"You were always *so* understanding," she sneered.

"All the same," he said, "it's not getting you anywhere. It isn't making you happy to stand in her way. Perhaps if you tried the other thing . . ."

"Oh, shut up! You're always preaching."

"Can't you realise how terribly hard it is on her?"

"It's been hard on me. I can't see that she has anything to whine about—it's time she learned that life isn't all fun. If she's so set on you, let her live with you and raise a brood of bastards . . ."

"Louise! Don't dare to talk like that!" He took a step towards her, his hands clenched.

She gave him a jeering smile. "You'd like to hit me, wouldn't you? Go on then, hit me—let's see how she likes you in jail. But you haven't the guts, have you? You never did have any guts. Nice, kind, understanding, tolerant Charles! Civilised Charles!"

"I think you must be mad."

"Such an active man—but hardly a man of action, eh, Charles? You prefer to write letters, don't you?—to put your case and try to make people see reason? You prefer to beg. Why don't you go down on your knees and plead for your popsy? Go on—crawl! I like it." She reached for her glass and drained it and lay back, mocking him. "The dirty little slut!"

For a second he almost lost control. He had never in his life felt towards anyone as he did at that moment towards her. He stood looking down at the ravaged face, the stringy throat, and the blood pounded in his head.

Then he turned away from her, shutting out the sight. He strode out of the room and across the narrow hall and out through the open front door without a word. He was trembling with anger. What a fool he'd been to come!

On days when he happened to be in the West End and Kathryn couldn't meet him he usually lunched at his club, the Colonial Services, where he had several good friends. Mechanically he drove in that direction now, but as he approached Pall Mall he knew that the last thing he wanted to do was to talk to anyone. Instead of going to the club therefore, he parked the car and walked through to Duncannon Street, where there was a pub he liked. He ordered a sandwich and a pint of mild-and-bitter and retired to a corner to cool off.

He still felt shaken by the violence of his rage, and not a little horrified at the impulse which he had so narrowly mastered. This business must be getting him down more than he'd realised. Louise had behaved abominably, but she was a psychological case if ever there was one. Obviously she had dwelt on her supposed grievances until they had become an obsession, and she could hardly be held accountable for what she'd said. He had been stupid to let himself be provoked. The best thing he could do now was to put her out of his mind altogether.

It would have been easier if he could have seen Kathryn at once and told her what had happened, but she was out on a job and wouldn't be free until the early evening. Meanwhile, he had to occupy himself. He could go back to his Hampstead flat and get on with his work, of course. He was writing a report on a subject which he found absorbing —the comparative productivity of six experimental small-holdings which he had set up in Trinidad and nursed to maturity before his retirement from the colonial service. The results, he believed, might lead to a revolution in small-scale husbandry in the Caribbean. But today he had no heart for it—after that disturbing interview, and with the problem of his and Kathryn's future still unsettled, he doubted his ability to concentrate. He lit his pipe and considered various ways of passing the time. Perhaps he'd go to the pictures . . .

He was still debating when a headline in someone's *Evening Standard* caught his eye. "England All Out," it said. Now that was an idea—he could go to the Oval. It was years since he had watched any first-class cricket, and he had heard that there were one or two spectacular batsmen in the Indian team. Anyhow, the weather was much more suited to cricket than the cinema.

He finished his beer and walked slowly back to the car. Now that cricket was decided on, he became preoccupied again with the fundamental problem of what he and Kathryn were going to do. Kathryn, of course, would say that Louise had settled the matter for them and that they must go ahead with their plans. It would be hard to resist her—and harder still to resist his own deep longing. All the same, he wished he could feel more confidence in the outcome.

It was just after two o'clock when he reached the Oval. There were so many "No Parking" signs near the ground that it took him a little time to find a street where he could leave the car. When he finally reached the entrance he discovered that all the stands were full—the Test Match and the fine day combined had drawn a huge crowd. He paid his four-and-six at the turnstile and edged his way around the field. He'd have to stand if he wanted to see anything, and even so it was going to be difficult to get a clear view. It was also going to be hot—perhaps after all he'd have done better in an air-conditioned cinema! Presently, though, he found a place where the crowd was a little sparser and came to a stop.

The cricket proved disappointingly dull. Runs were coming at an incredibly slow rate, and there was an air of lethargy about the game most inappropriate to a Test Match. Perhaps the heat was responsible. For a while he made an effort to follow the play, but gradually his attention wandered and his thoughts turned inwards again. It was all very well to tell himself that he must put Louise out of his mind, but the picture of her hate-distorted face kept obtruding itself against his will. If only he could convince himself that he had no responsibility for the frightful state she had got into! There must have been a fundamental defect of character in the first place, otherwise she would never have allowed herself to go to pieces as she had done, but might she not have fared better in different circumstances? After all, she had been doing quite well as a model in London, and if he hadn't married her she would probably have met some well-to-do man who would have been happy to devote himself to an attractive good-time girl. Then all this might never have happened. Instead, she had been snatched away from the environment she was used to and plunged into a new and strange one. Had he taken the risks of transplantation sufficiently into account? The initiative had certainly been his—he had urged and persuaded her to go with him. He had tried to put the facts squarely, but he had still persuaded her. He had deliberately set out to reshape her life to the pattern of his own—and he couldn't deny that. So hadn't he a responsibility?

And when the experiment failed—had he been fair to her? He didn't know—he honestly didn't know. It seemed pretty hard that a man should be expected to give up his life's work for the sake of a wife who had said so soon after her marriage that she didn't care for him—that she despised him.   She could have come back to England alone if she had wanted to—he would gladly have provided for her, and she could have made a fresh start.   The decision to stay had been her own.   But did that absolve him? Having taken her for better or for worse, shouldn't he have brought her home himself, away from the heat and the rum, when he saw how demoralised she was getting?   Hadn't it been his duty to get her out of it at whatever sacrifice to himself?

Or were these the morbid self-questionings of a man suffering from nervous strain and the shock of an unpleasant encounter . . .?

He glanced apathetically at his scorecard as the fall of a wicket brought a stir of interest among the spectators. He had only the vaguest idea of what had been going on, and suddenly it seemed rather absurd that he should be standing here in the blazing sun when he couldn't keep his mind on the game for two consecutive minutes.   He'd be better off at home—it would be hours yet before he could see Kathryn.   He waited until the new batsman was settled in, but when the play showed no sign of picking up he decided to call it a day and threaded his way back through the anonymous throng to the exit.

CHAPTER II

"In fact, Sir John," Kathryn Forrester said, "We need many more policemen. That's the answer, isn't it?"

She was sitting in a deck-chair on the lawn outside Sir John Fawcett's country home, thoughtfully turning the pages of the book of reminiscences which was to be the basis of her forthcoming television interview with the retired Commissioner of Police.

"That's it," he agreed. "And if the public want law and order to be maintained they've got to make police conditions sufficiently attractive to bring in enough of the right sort of men."

"Well, that should be a good note to end on . . ." Kathryn turned the book sideways and examined one of the photographs. "You know, I'm wondering if it mightn't be a good idea to break up our conversation with actual film shots of some of the things we'll be talking about. For instance, the police and the miners playing football together during the General Strike . . ."

"That would be splendid. Would you be able to get hold of the film?"

"I expect it could be managed. We've quite a collection of old cinema newsreels in the Film Library, and we can usually borrow what we haven't got ourselves. I'll see what I can find." She picked up her bag and gloves.

"Won't you have another cup of tea before you go?" Fawcett sounded genuinely reluctant to let her leave. The fact was that he had taken a great liking to this efficient young woman with the piquant face and the warm brown eyes,

"No more, thank you, Sir John—I really must get back to the studio. I'll see you on Wednesday, then, for rehearsal."

"On Wednesday at ten. I'm afraid I'm going to be horribly nervous."

She looked with some amusement at the strong features

and tall upright figure of the man who had spent his life in the suppression of crime. "You don't look as though you could ever be afraid of anything. *I* think you're going to be a great success."

"At least it will be a novel experience. Will there be a chance, do you suppose, of my being able to look over the place while I'm there? I'd very much like to."

"Why, of course. I'll be glad to show you round after rehearsal."

"That's extremely kind of you." Fawcett strolled with her across the lawn and opened the door of her car. "Well, it's been delightful to meet you, Miss Forrester. I've seen you on television so often that I felt I knew you before you came, but a picture is never quite as good as the real thing, is it?"

She laughed. "That rather depends on the real thing. Good-bye, Sir John." She gave him a friendly wave and shot quickly away down the broad gravel drive.

Kathryn was fortunate in having found a job that suited her perfectly. At one time she had wanted to be an actress, and had put in a year's hard work at the Royal Academy of Dramatic Art before realising that her talent was not sufficiently unusual to offer much of a prospect in such an overcrowded profession. Then she had switched to newspaper reporting, first in the provinces and afterwards in Fleet Street, but again she had been competent rather than brilliant. She had enjoyed the interviewing, but she had never been very good at the rough-and-tumble assignments that were inseparable from general reporting. Television had given her just the medium she needed. To become a successful compère in a popular magazine programme you had to be able to organise a bit, and act a bit, and talk to people easily in front of the cameras, and of course look nice, and she could do all those things. She had found her niche.

Professionally speaking, she felt very content as she swung the car into the London road after seeing the ex-Commissioner. These preliminary interviews didn't always turn out so well. Though she had a natural friendliness which was an enormous asset in her job, some people took a great deal of breaking down, and with a thirty-minute programme to put on every fortnight there were limits to the time she could devote to each individual. But Sir John had been the perfect subject—direct in his manner, clear-cut in his views, and eager to co-operate. He was going to be very photogenic, too, with his crisp silver hair and fine head. At twenty-nine, Kathryn preferred maturity to youthful good looks—which was just as well, she reflected, since Charles wouldn't see forty again.

Her thoughts took a familiar path back to the interview that had started it all, nearly two years ago now, when she had called on Charles Hilary at his London hotel and he had talked to her about the problem of feeding-stuffs in Antigua! It had been an odd start to a romance, but he hadn't been so solemn at rehearsal, and by the time they'd faced the cameras together they'd both wanted to go on meeting. It was natural enough, she supposed—nurses often married their patients, after all, and television interviewers were a bit like nurses, encouraging and sustaining their subjects . . . Only, in their case, they hadn't married.

A cloud settled on her face. What a hopeless situation they'd got into! They'd reached a point where being together wasn't much fun any more, they were both so tense and strained. That stupid quarrel she had started last night!—sheer nerves, of course, but if they had many more scenes like that everything would go sour on them. Poor Charles! Still, he'd have to get over those scruples of his and make a decision. In the end he would, of course —she hadn't a doubt about it, or about what the decision would be. But why wait? She wondered how he'd fared with Louise, and her foot pressed down harder on the accelerator.

It was nearly six when she reached the studio. She cleared up one or two things on her desk and had a word with her producer about the way the next programme was shaping. Then she went along to the Film Library to see if Bob Sanderson could help her with pictures.

Bob was a lanky adolescent whose job—a menial one, in his view—was to file away enormous quantities of film in flat circular tin boxes according to the instructions of his chief, Mr. Sprott, and stand by in the evenings in case anyone should want something suddenly. Unlike Kathryn, he was a square peg in a round hole. His passion was sport —as a participant, when he could manage it, and vicariously when he couldn't. His ambition was to become a sports writer, like his friend Leslie Holmes on the *Record*. His nose was buried in the back page of the *Star* when Kathryn looked in.

"Hallo, Bob—you don't seem very busy."

He whipped his feet off the table when he saw who it was. He had got over the worst of his calf-love for Kathryn, but he still thought she was smashing.

"Quiet as the grave," he said sepulchrally. He was having a little trouble with his lower register.

"Well, here's something that's right up your street." She sat down at the table and opened Fawcett's book, *A Policeman Looks Back*. "Do you think you could find some film showing police and miners playing football together during the General Strike?"

He took the book from her and examined the photograph. "I never heard about that."

"It was before your time."

He grinned. "I'll have a look, Grandma, anyway. Is that all?"

"No, I want something about those Irishmen who put bombs in the Underground—I.R.A."

"You don't expect an action picture of that?"

"I'm not fussy—any bit of destruction will do."

"All right. Do you want to see them now?"

"Not specially. Just put them aside, and you can run them through for me on Monday evening. I shall only want about thirty seconds of each."

He nodded. "I say, have you seen any of the Wimbledon stuff lately?"

"No, I've been up to my eyes."

"Well, have a look at this." He switched on a projector and a picture appeared on a small screen at the end of the room. It was the Centre Court. People were sitting with newspapers folded over their heads to keep the sun off and looked as though they were being slowly fried. Behind them an indicator showed that Miss Maureen Connolly was leading her opponent by three games to two in the second set. The camera switched to a sturdy young woman who at once lashed a ball with devastating precision into the farthest corner of the court.

"'Little Mo'," said Bob, in a tone of hushed hero-worship. "Isn't she super?"

"She's very attractive," Kathryn agreed.

"Don't be silly—I'm talking about her backhand drive. Gosh, what wouldn't I give to have a follow-through like that!"

They watched an exciting rally or two. Then Kathryn said: "Wonderful—but I really must run."

Bob switched off. 'Okay, Kathryn, I'll have the stuff by Monday. So long."

She smiled her thanks and went quickly back to her room to collect her belongings.

A few minutes later she was on her way to her Chelsea flat. The rush-hour traffic had thinned and she drove fast, with hardly any checks. She parked the car on an empty bomb-site that she often used as a garage and had just changed her clothes when the telephone rang. It was Charles, to see if she were back. Twenty minutes later she heard his double hoot outside and went to let him in.

He took her into his arms with a grateful sigh, resting his cheek against her thick dark hair and holding her very tight. For a moment they kissed and clung together in a fervour of unspoken reconciliation.

Then he said ruefully. "I'd better tell you at once, darling—it didn't work. It was just like hammering on a brick wall. I didn't make the slightest impression."

She felt hardly a trace of disappointment, for it was only what she had expected. "Oh, well," she said, "come and have a drink." She poured sherry while he fumbled with his pipe and tobacco pouch. "Have you just come from her"?

"Lord, no—I saw her before lunch and it was all over inside half an hour. I've been kicking my heels ever since. I couldn't work and I didn't feel fit company for anyone so in the end I went to the Oval and watched a bit of the Test Match."

She handed him his drink. "That was a good idea. Did you enjoy it?"

"Not really. There was a shocking crowd—the only place I could squeeze in was by the scoreboard and you never get much of a view from there. Besides, the play was very slow . . ." He caught her reproachful look and suddenly felt ashamed. "I'm sorry, darling, I'm afraid I'm in a vile mood . . . How did you get on with Fawcett?"

"Oh, he's a lamb. We hit it off perfectly."

"I suppose that means you've made another conquest. You're collecting quite an empire!"

"Which only shows how wonderful *you* must be." Kathryn put her glass down. "Come on, darling, what happened—can you bear to tell me?"

"There isn't much to tell. She said 'No'—that's all. She's skin deep in everything but hate, but that goes right to her marrow. Apparently she's been seeing you looking glamorous on TV and now she's got it in for you as well as for me. She's not just stubborn, the way she used to be—she's bitter. I'd say that preventing you and me marrying is about the one thing that keeps her going. She's making it her life's work."

"Oh, Charles, isn't it wicked? Really, the law's monstrous . . . ! What was she like—was she sober?"

"Sober enough to know what she was saying—to start with, anyhow. She got very abusive towards the end—really nasty. It was all I could do to keep my hands off her."

"Now you're exaggerating."

"No, I mean it. It just shows the effect she's having on me—for a few seconds I literally saw red. It quite shook me."

"I suppose it was a mistake to go—I'm to blame for that, aren't I?"

"It was my idea."

"I know, but I did rather drive you to it."

"Oh, well, we were both rattled last night—and small wonder! Anyhow, we had to make sure. I hated going, but I'm glad I went. One thing's quite certain now—divorce is ruled right out. There's not a hope that she'll change her mind."

"Did you say anything about divorcing *her*?"

"Yes, but she only laughed and said we'd never get any evidence. In any case it would take ages to prove anything, and we still might not be successful in the end."

Kathryn lit a cigarette. "Well, there it is. We've done our best—now there's nothing for it but to put Plan B into operation."

"I still think it's a hell of a step to take," said Charles gloomily

"It is a big step, of course, but we've got to take it."

"It's your being so well-known that's the trouble. If two ordinary people decide to live together as man and wife when they're not, the chances are that no one will know or care. But when one of them's by way of being a celebrity . . ."

"We'll be living abroad, don't forget."

"Yes, I know, but the newspapers are bound to wonder what's happened to you and sooner or later someone will recognise you. I can just imagine the sort of publicity there'll be then."

"Oh, Charles, really! Anyone would think we hadn't been over all this a thousand times already. You know how quickly people forget faces."

"Not yours!"

"Darling, you *are* being difficult. I tell you it simply doesn't matter. We shall be living our own life—we'll probably never even see an English newspaper. We'll find a nice quiet spot somewhere in France, in the south, with a little terrace and a gorgeous view, and you can get on with your book and I'll prune the vines or whatever one does to them and we won't bother what anyone thinks at all."

"It sounds idyllic, the way you put it. But how long would it be, I wonder, before you found yourself missing the life you lead here, with all your friends and the excitement you're used to? Your work means a lot to you, after all, and you've the prospect of a fine career . . ."

She interrupted him impatiently. "Now look, Charles, we've discussed all this before—every bit of it. What's the matter with you? Are you getting cold feet?"

"Not on my own account—it's you that I'm worried about. More worried than I was yesterday. Don't you see, Kathryn, how history is repeating itself? I didn't realise it fully until Louise accused me today of ruining her life . . ."

"That is simply not true."

"Perhaps not—but the fact remains that I did persuade her to go away with me and live my sort of life—or try to—and it didn't work out. That's the thought that's been gnawing at me all day. God knows I want us to be together more than anything else in the world—but suppose it

22

does not work out this time, either? I don't think I'd ever forgive myself."

Kathryn's expression softened. "My darling, there's absolutely no comparison. For one thing, I'm older than she was and more experienced, and I'm a lot more sensible. I know exactly what I'm doing. I won't pretend that I don't enjoy my job, and if we could marry and have a family and I could go on working in between it would be heavenly. But we can't, so there's no point in dwelling on that. And if it's a choice between the job and you, I prefer you. Don't you see, darling—the job doesn't mean anything without you. Nothing does. I know it's good-bye to the sort of life I've been used to, and the beginning of an entirely different one, but that's the way I want it."

He sighed, still not quite daring to believe her. "You're a remarkable woman, Kathryn."

"There's nothing remarkable about me, darling. I'm just like any other woman who's in love. What I want more than anything is a home with you and a share in your work and—in the end—our children." She looked up at him with a smile. "And if you turn me down after that I'll never speak to you again!"

He held her close. "I want it too, my love. That's the trouble—I want it so much that I'm afraid of spoiling things."

"The only way we can spoil things is by doing nothing. We can't go on as we are. It was all right to start with, when we were so new to each other and a snatched week-end was bliss, but that's nearly two years ago. It's gone too far now, Char _s. Having the cottage and the boat is all very well, but it's only a makeshift and you know it. I'm tired of living separately all the week for the sake of appearances. I know I can't stand it much longer and I don't believe you can either. We've got to go on together—really together—or we've got to break it up, and we know we can't break it up because we've tried."

He nodded slowly. "Yes, that's all true . . . Well, what do you suggest we do?"

"I shall send in my resignation on Monday. I'm under contract for three more programmes and of course I'll have to do those, but by the middle of August I'll be free. There's absolutely no point in our hanging about, so I suggest we scrap the holiday we'd planned in Peter's boat, and go to France instead. And we'll concentrate on finding somewhere to live."

She seemed so confident, so determined, that his last doubts were resolved. "All right, my love," he said, "I'll drop Peter a line tonight and tell him we shan't be needing *Witch* after all. That will make a start."

"Angel!"

"With a bit of luck, we should be able to get fixed up comfortably before the winter."

"With a bit of luck," she said, "we'll forget what winters are like. Oh, Charles, it's going to be so wonderful."

He took her face in his hands. "I love you, Kathryn. I'll always love you. I hope I'll make you happy." He kissed her tenderly. Then he gave a long sigh of thankfulness, as though a great burden had rolled away. "I say, why don't we go to Pedro's and celebrate?"

"Now you're talking!" said Kathryn. "Just give me two minutes."

CHAPTER III

CHARLES was still under the spell of their new happiness when, just before ten next morning, he turned his car into the forecourt of the big block in Hampstead where he lived. He parked beside a blue Austin in which two men were sitting talking and walked briskly through the hallway, nodding a cheerful "Good morning" to the porter. The day was perfect and he felt on top of the world. Kathryn had had to go into the office for an hour or two but at noon he would be calling for her and they would be on their way to the cottage, brimming with plans and no longer caring whether anyone saw them or not. Anxiety seemed a thing of the past.

He unlocked the door of his flat and was about to go in when footsteps sounded behind him and a voice said, "Excuse me, sir—are you by any chance Charles Hilary?"

He turned sharply, and saw that the two men from the Austin had followed him in. One was a tall, youngish man, with a fresh complexion; the other was older, with heavy shoulders and grizzled brows and moustache. They were both wearing navy suits and soft felt hats and they looked quietly formidable.

"Yes," he said, "I'm Charles Hilary."

"Then I'd very much like a word with you," said the older of the two. "My name is Bates—Chief-Inspector Bates of the C.I.D."

Charles stared at him in surprise. "Well, you'd better come in," he said after a moment. He collected his morning paper from the letter-box and led the way inside. "What's the trouble, Inspector?"

"It's about your wife, sir—Mrs. Louise Hilary."

Charles became very still. "Oh, yes?"

"You haven't heard the news?" The inspector's voice had an undertone of scepticism.

25

"What news? I've heard nothing."

"I see. Well, I'm sorry to have to tell you, sir, that your wife has been found dead."

"Dead!" Charles met the inspector's scrutiny with shocked eyes. "Good God! When? Where?"

"Yesterday afternoon, at her house in Clandon Mews. She was strangled."

"*Strangled!*" In horror he gazed first at one policeman, then at the other. "You can't mean that—there must be some mistake."

Unemotionally, the second man picked up the unopened newspaper from the settee, folded it back, and held it out with his thumb on a four-line paragraph headed "Woman Found Strangled." Charles read it incredulously.

"Oh, my God!" he said, and sat down. He felt sick. Into his mind there had come the picture of Louise lying back on her couch, taunting him. He saw again the thin neck that he had wanted to choke the life out of in that moment of almost ungovernable anger. In spirit, for those brief seconds, he had been a murderer himself—and now she was dead, *strangled*. It was horrible—it seemed uncanny.

The inspector's voice broke into his thoughts. "We found a letter in the bedroom, Mr. Hilary, which appeared to have come from you." His tone could hardly have been more accusing if it had been a bomb they had discovered.

With the clarity of revelation, Charles suddenly saw the danger in which he stood. If they'd found the letter they knew about his desperate state of mind, about the divorce that Louise had refused, about Kathryn. It seemed fantastic, but they had grounds for suspecting *him* of the murder. That was why they had been waiting for him. He met their cold, convergent gaze and his mind recoiled from the question he knew was inevitable.

"Your letter indicated that you wanted to see her urgently. You didn't, I suppose, see her yesterday?"

For a split second, Charles wavered between the invited "No", the incriminating "Yes". Time—that was what he needed—time to think. To say "No" might let him out straight away, but to say "Yes"—what would that involve him in? Explanations, protestations—and they might still not believe him. God, they might even think that Kathryn had been concerned . . .

"No," he said sharply, "I didn't see her yesterday. I *had* wanted to, as a matter of fact, but when I rang her up early in the morning she told me she was going away and would have to pack . . ." Once the lie was told, words came pouring out to bolster it. He looked more confidently at Bates. "Surely, Inspector, you don't imagine that *I* had anything to do with this?"

"I'm not imagining anything, sir," Bates said. "I'm merely seeking information. When, in fact, *did* you last see your wife?"

"Oh, quite a long time ago—early in May, I think."

Bates nodded, and glanced at his notebook. The tension seemed to ease a little. It's all right, Charles thought—they won't be able to prove I was there. There was no one about when I went to the flat—not near enough to identify me, anyhow. And I didn't do it, so there's no need to worry. But his heart continued to beat violently, so that it seemed to him the two men couldn't fail to hear it.

"Well, sir," said the inspector, after a pause, "perhaps you can give me a little help. Do you happen to know anything about your wife's relationships with other people? Other—men?"

"I doubt if there's much I can tell you about that . . . Oh, there was one thing . . ." He mentioned the taxi incident in Piccadilly. "But I couldn't describe the man," he said. "I only saw his back."

Bates was visibly unimpressed. "You know of no—friendship? No liaison? She never mentioned anyone?"

"No, Inspector. I'm afraid my wife had become almost a stranger to me. We've been living in separate establishments for nearly two years, you see, and we rarely met."

"Quite so." Bates gave a little cough. "As a matter of interest, sir, what *were* you doing yesterday afternoon?"

"I was at the Oval, watching the cricket."

"With a companion?"

"No, alone."

"H'm. I wonder if you'd mind giving me a rough idea

of your time-table from lunch-time onwards. Pure routine, you understand—we have to ask these questions."

"I realise that, of course . . . Well, now, let me think . . ." Briefly, he told how he had dropped into the pub for a beer and a sandwich and how he'd suddenly got the idea that he'd like to see the Test Match. "I drove down just before two o'clock and went into the ground soon after the resumption of play—say, twenty past two. I stayed till about a quarter to four, and then came home."

"Yes, I see." Bates glanced at his colleague. "All right, Mr. Hilary, I think that's all for the moment—except that I'd feel obliged if you'd let Sergeant Nixon here take your finger-prints."

Finger-prints! For a moment Charles gaped at the inspector. That was something he had completely overlooked. They would go over the house for fingerprints, of course—and they would find his! They would find them on the bottle of rum and on the glass he had handed to Louise. They would know that he had been at the house yesterday—they would know that he had lied. And what could he say? He stood aghast at the enormity of his blunder.

"Well, sir?"

Desperately he tried to repair the damage. "Look, Inspector, I—I'm afraid I misled you. I *was* at my wife's house yesterday—but not in the afternoon, in the morning. I left her before one o'clock and I swear I didn't see her again."

The grey eyes of Inspector Bates had become very cold. "Why didn't you tell me this in the first place?"

"Because I saw what a frightful position I was in. I'm sorry—it was an idiotic thing to do. I realise that now."

"Now that circumstances have compelled you to admit the truth, you mean?"

Charles took a deep breath. "The truth is that I did not kill my wife. She was alive when I left her. But you'd read that letter, and you made it plain enough that you suspected me. The fact that I happened to be with her in the morning had nothing to do with her death, but I thought you would draw the wrong conclusions if I told you I'd been there."

Bates grunted. "Well, I shall have to ask you to accompany me to the station, I'm afraid."

"You mean you're arresting me?"

"No, sir, I'm not arresting you, but in view of what's happened we shall have to know a great deal more about your movements and it will be more convenient at the station. Have you any objection?"

"You're on the wrong track, Inspector, I can tell you that, but I don't mind coming with you if you think it will help you to get at the truth." Charles turned unhappily towards the door. He felt dazed by the speed of events—it seemed hardly possible that he could have got into such a mess in so short a time. He wondered how long it would take to sort things out. It didn't look as though he would be able to keep his appointment with Kathryn and that meant that she would be ringing the flat to find out what had happened. He stopped in the entrance hall and left a message for her with the porter—that he'd been suddenly called away and would be telephoning her. Then he stepped out into the bright sunshine, with the two policemen close behind him.

Sitting back in the car, with the stolid inspector at his side, it occurred to him that perhaps he ought to ask for a lawyer to be present at the resumed interview. Yet that was necessary, surely, only when a man had something to hide and might give his case away by talking too freely? As an innocent suspect, his own best course was obviously to be frank about everything, and he needed no help in that respect. He dismissed the idea.

His thoughts turned to Louise, and he wondered how she had really met her death. She had been getting pretty drunk when he had left her and she had probably gone on drinking. If some man she knew had called in the afternoon she might easily have provoked a fatal quarrel. What a sordid, ghastly business!

The car came to a stop and Bates led the way into the station and round the back to a small room with a table and several hard chairs. Then he disappeared for a while, leaving Charles with the unloquacious Sergeant Nixon. When he returned he had another plain-clothes man with him, who sat down at the table with a large notebook.

Bates cleared his throat. "Well, sir, as I told you you're not under arrest, but considering all the circumstances I think perhaps I ought to tell you that you're not obliged to say anything, and that anything you do say will be taken down and may be used in evidence in any subsequent proceedings. Is that quite clear?"

"Quite clear, Inspector. I want to be completely open with you—I've nothing whatever to conceal."

"Perhaps you'll tell me, then, in your own words, exactly what took place yesterday morning?"

With a feeling of relief, Charles began to unburden himself. He told of his telephone call to Louise, of how he had suggested an afternoon visit and she had preferred the morning, of his arrival by car before lunch, and of their conversation. As though to make amends for his earlier deception, he was absolutely frank about the angry scene they had had, and the reason for it, and the terms on which they had parted. The shorthand writer's pen moved swiftly over the pages. Bates heard him out in silence, and then began to put questions.

"Did you happen to mention to anyone else that you were going to pay this visit in the morning?"

Charles shook his head. Kathryn had known he was going, of course, but she hadn't known when, and anyhow the last thing he wanted to do was to bring her into it.

"Did you stop anywhere on your way from your flat to the mews?"

"No."

"Did you park your car in the mews?"

"No, a little way down the road on the other side."

"Why did you do that?"

"It was a very hot morning and that was the nearest bit of shade."

"I see. Do you think anyone saw you as you approached the mews, or as you left it?"

"I rather doubt it," said Charles ruefully, remembering how he had been congratulating himself on the fact only a short time ago. "I wasn't paying much attention because I was thinking about what I was going to say to my wife, but I don't recall seeing anyone. I suppose I just happened to hit a quiet part of the day."

"H'm. Now what about after you left the mews? You say you went to this pub in Duncannon Street. How long were you there?"

"About half an hour."

"Would anyone there remember you, do you think?"

"I imagine the barman would. He knows me by sight."

"But he wouldn't know where you'd come from, of course?"

"No."

"Did you happen to mention to him or anyone else where you thought of going?"

"No."

"When you got to the Oval, did you put your car in the car park?"

"No, it was full up. I drove around looking for a quiet street and parked it by the kerb with a lot of others."

"Can you remember the name of the street?"

"No, but I could find it again."

"Did you happen to notice what cars were near yours? Make, colour, any details about them?"

Charles pressed the palm of his hand against his forehead. "No, I—I'm afraid not. I wasn't really in the mood to notice anything—that's the trouble."

"What part of the ground did you go into—one of the enclosures?"

"No, they were all full—the whole place was pretty packed. I went in with the crowd, and even so I had quite a job to find standing room."

Nixon intervened. "Did you buy a scorecard?"

"Yes."

"Did you keep it?"

Charles frowned. "No, I don't think I did. I seem to remember screwing it up and throwing it away just before I left."

The pen flowed on. Nixon studied his nails.

"Did you speak to anyone during the afternoon?" Bates resumed. "Anyone who might remember you?"

"No, Inspector. I wasn't in a very chatty frame of mind." Charles was beginning to feel the strain.

"You do realise how important it is to establish that you were actually there?"

"Of course I do. I wish I could think of something."

"At least you can describe the game."

Charles hesitated. "I'll try, but I don't pretend to be an expert on cricket. I was only killing time."

Bates savoured the phrase. "Killing—time?"

"Yes, Inspector. I had an engagement in the evening but nothing to do until then, and I thought the game might occupy my mind."

"Let's see if it did. Just tell us what you remember."

"Well, India were batting, of course . . ."

"Who were the batsmen when you arrived?"

"Oh—er—Chandri was one. I'm not quite sure about the other—those Indian names don't stay in the mind. I think it began with Man . . ."

"Manjdirar?" suggested Nixon.

"I think so," said Charles doubtfully.

"Or Mankari?" The sergeant was evidently a keen follower of the game.

"I'm not absolutely sure."

"You had a scorecard," Nixon reminded him.

"I know, but I was—well, I was just watching the scene, getting a general impression. I enjoy cricket for the strokes, not for the players."

"What about the bowlers?" asked Bates.

"Oh—Holt and—Newman, I think. To start with."

"All right. Now if you could just describe what you can remember of the game—any incidents, any excitement, any wickets taken, changes of bowler and so on . . ."

For fifteen minutes Charles groped painfully in his memory while Bates took him through the afternoon's play. It was a gruelling examination, and he knew he wasn't doing very well. Several times Nixon gave an audible sniff, and once, unnervingly, he took a newspaper from his pocket and referred to it.

"Well, there it is," said Charles at last. "I'm afraid it's not much of an account, but it's the best I can do. The fact is, I wasn't concentrating most of the time. My mind was on other things."

"You still insist you were there?" said Bates gravely.

"I was there."

"And you still maintain that you didn't go to Clandon Mews in the afternoon?"

"I didn't go near the place. After I left the Oval I

drove straight home and stayed there until the early evening."

At that moment there was a tap at the door and the inspector was called to the telephone. The shorthand writer closed his book and sat back. Nixon avoided Charles's eye and gazed out of the window. Charles wondered if Kathryn had rung yet, and what she had made of the porter's message. The police seemed to have exhausted their questions but they would probably want him to sign something and it would take a long time to type all that stuff out. . . .

Then Bates returned. "Well, Mr. Hilary," he said briskly, "there's been a development—quite a piece of luck. We've found a woman who says she saw a man leave your wife's flat in Clandon Mews about half past three yesterday afternoon and she thinks she might be able to identify him."

"Thank God for that!" Charles exclaimed. "I told you I had nothing to do with it, Inspector. Now you'll see that I've been telling the truth."

"I'm sure I hope so, sir." The inspector's manner had become much milder. "Perhaps you wouldn't mind attending an identification parade straight away and then I shan't need to trouble you any more." He explained the procedure.

"Right!" said Charles eagerly. "Let's get it over."

There were several men already waiting in the yard of Gate Street police station when Charles joined them, and others were being shepherded in from the city pavements to do their civic duty. Most of them were of about Charles's own age and physical stamp, and all were hatless. Soon there were eleven besides himself.

After a few minutes Bates appeared and asked them to form a line against the wall. Then the woman was brought out. She was of medium height, quietly dressed, and about forty years old. Her pleasant face wore a rather serious expression. She walked quickly along the row, giving only the briefest glance at each face. But opposite Charles, she stopped.

"That's the man," she said, after the merest trace of hesitation.

Charles stared at her in horror. "Why, I've never seen you before in my life. . . ."

"But I've seen you," she said.

There was a moment's silence. Eleven men cast curious glances at Charles. Then Nixon took the woman away and the line broke up.

Charles felt a hand tighten on his arm. "Better come inside," said Bates.

CHAPTER IV

"CHARLES EDWARD HILARY, you are charged on indictment that on the 3rd day of June in this year you murdered Louise Mary Hilary. Charles Edward Hilary, are you guilty or not guilty?"

"Not guilty."

From the Old Bailey dock, Charles caught and returned Kathryn's phantom smile. At least, the waiting was almost over. It wouldn't be long now before they knew.

Seven weeks had dragged by since his arrest—seven weeks into which a lifetime of anxiety had been compressed. At first his chief feeling had been one of incredulity that he could actually be in prison on a murder charge—that this experience, which one only read about, could have happened to him. The whole thing, he had felt sure, was a horrible, stupid mistake and it was only a question of time before the police would be led to the real murderer and he would be released. Then, as talks with his solicitor and counsel had brought home the gravity of his position, keener emotions had assailed him. Anger at the monstrous injustice of it all. Corroding resentment at the trick that Fate had played on Kathryn and himself, shattering their lives at the moment of fulfilment. Anguish at the thought of what Kathryn must be going through. Chilling loneliness in the long nights. And starker feelings—shameful spasms of self-pity, and hot waves of fear when his imagination took control. Hope, despair, and hope again—and everything dagger sharp.

Now, as he listened to the jury being empanelled, incredulity returned. It seemed fantastic beyond belief that the purpose of all this ceremony was to weigh and judge *his* guilt, when in fact he knew no more about Louise's death

35

than the usher did. It was even more unbelievable that in a few hours or days these strangers who were now being sworn in might solemnly decide that he had killed his wife; that, innocent as the judge himself, he might hear a hideous sentence pronounced upon him and be sent to a place of execution to have his neck broken.

Unbelievable—yet here he undoubtedly was, the prisoner in the dock, the cause and focal point of one of the most publicised trials that the Old Bailey had seen for many years. He might feel detached from all the busy preparations, he might find them unreal, but there was nothing unreal about the policeman standing stiffly behind him, or about the expectant murmur from the gallery, or about the reporters already making descriptive notes of his appearance and demeanour. And there would be nothing unreal about the rope.

He moistened his lips and gazed nervously around the court. The crowd that had packed the public benches must be only a fraction of the mob that had failed to get in. It was because of Kathryn, of course, that the queue had begun to form at five; because of Kathryn that the newspapers were preparing to sell extra editions and the case was a topic of conversation in every corner of the country. She had been almost like another member of the family to hundreds of thousands of television viewers, so it wasn't surprising that people should be interested—but it was hateful to think what they must be saying. At least, if they expected juicy, intimate revelations about their fallen idol, they were going to be disappointed. That was one advantage of not having much of a defence—the prosecution could afford to be gentlemanly. According to Murgatroyd, there wouldn't be much drama or excitement about the trial. It would be over very quickly—and there wasn't a lot of hope. He had made that very clear.

As Charles looked up at the gallery, eyes focused on his face with avid curiosity. Only Kathryn, sitting beside her brother in the body of the court, met his glance with a message of assurance. She was pale, dreadfully pale, but as calm and sustaining as she had been all through. It seemed to Charles that he had not gauged her real calibre until now. He prayed that she would be given strength and courage in the racking hours that lay ahead.

36

Sir Francis Duke, Q.C., patted his wig, hitched up his gown, and rose majestically.

"May it please your Lordship! I appear in this case on behalf of the Crown with my learned friend Mr. Forbes. The prisoner, Charles Hilary, has the advantage of being represented by my learned friends Mr. Leo Murgatroyd and Mr. Hollis . . ."

Duke made an excellent prosecuting counsel. He was a big, solid man, with the sort of presence that inspires confidence in juries. His outlook on life was somewhat conventional and narrow, but he wasn't the kind of bigot who would seek to hang a man for adultery if he couldn't hang him for murder. He could be relied upon to put the Crown case fully and effectively, while still conceding whatever was proper to the other side. There was nothing spectacular about his methods, nothing at all magnetic about his personality, but then this case called for no special brilliance—not on the prosecution side. The facts would speak eloquently enough for themselves.

"Members of the jury," he began. "At about a quarter to four on the afternoon of Friday, June 3rd, the body of Louise Hilary was discovered in the sitting-room of her house at 1 Clandon Mews, Kensington, where she lived alone. The discovery was made by a messenger boy, Arthur Mason, who had called to deliver a railway ticket from the Wide World Travel Agency. Getting no reply to his knock, and having been told that Mrs. Hilary was expecting him, he peered through the vertical slit of the letter-box to see if there was any sign of her. To his horror he saw a pair of legs outstretched upon the sitting-room floor in an attitude which plainly indicated that something was amiss. He went at once to a nearby telephone box and dialled 999. The police arrived a few minutes later, forced the door, and found that Louise Hilary was dead. She had been strangled.

"Now it has been possible to establish, within comparatively narrow limits, at what time this murder was committed. Shortly before three-fifteen that afternoon Louise Hilary made a telephone call to the Wide World Travel Agency asking what had happened about the ticket for Paris which she had ordered. Her voice was recognised by a clerk, William Harbin, who had dealt with her travel requirements on a number of previous occasions. We can therefore say with certainty that she was alive at a quarter past three. By a quarter to four, the recorded time of the messenger boy's 999 call, she was dead. She had been murdered within those thirty minutes. The absence of any signs of forcible entry at the house shows that the murderer was admitted by Louise Hilary herself and that he was therefore an acceptable visitor. In the submission of the prosecution, there can be no doubt who that visitor was. During the course of a routine search of the premises, the police discovered on a bottle of rum in the sitting-room and on a glass from which Louise Hilary had been drinking, several clear finger-prints which were subsequently identified as those of her husband, Charles Hilary. The most painstaking investigations by the police have failed to produce any evidence that any other man was present in the house that afternoon.

"Members of the jury, those finger-prints were not the only discovery. On Louise Hilary's bed a letter was found —a letter from her husband which had been posted just before midnight and which she had evidently received that morning. You will be able to study this letter, which is being put in evidence by the prosecution. For the moment, I think it will suffice if I read aloud two or three paragraphs. In passing I would draw your attention to the fact that, Hilary addresses his wife simply as 'Louise!'—his attitude to her being such, apparently, that he could not bring himself to what after all is no more than a formality—the word 'Dear'. Now here are the relevant portions of the letter:

"'I can't believe you realise what unhappiness you are causing by your continued refusal to divorce me. I can neither work nor sleep for trying to think of some way out of the impasse—it occupies my mind to the exclusion of everything else. Kathryn feels it even more than I do. She naturally wants a home and children and a normal life and cannot bear any longer the hole-and-corner liaison which you have forced on us.

"'If you yourself had any love for me, I could understand your refusal to set me free, but you made it plain even before we separated that our disastrous marriage

38

had left you with feelings only of dislike. What, then, do you gain by holding out?—what conceivable good can it do you to put this obstacle in my way?

"'Louise, I am desperate—so desperate that I find it difficult to write with restraint. You are destroying my life. If I could see you and talk to you again perhaps I could make you understand what you are doing. I'll ring you in the morning to find out whether I can come tomorrow.'"

Sir Francis laid the document down and dabbed his mouth with the corner of a white handkerchief. "'Tomorrow', ladies and gentlemen, was the day of the murder."

He paused and regarded the jury across the hushed court. "In the light of what happened afterwards, it would be difficult to imagine a more damning letter. The prosecution is not required to prove a motive in order to establish the guilt of the prisoner, but here a motive stares us in the face. Consider the situation that this letter discloses. Charles Hilary, after an unhappy marriage, is living apart from his wife. He has fallen passionately in love with a certain 'Kathryn', whom we now know to be Miss Kathryn Forrester, an attractive television artist. He has made her his mistress and is anxious to marry her. He has several times asked his wife for a divorce, but she has always refused. The strain of the 'hole-and-corner liaison', the knowledge that there is no future in it, has become intolerable, and Kathryn Forrester has declared that she cannot stand the situation any longer. Hilary must secure a divorce, or perhaps lose the woman he loves. His state of mind is desperate, and in that state of mind he visits his wife. None of this is in dispute.

"What happened during that meeting we cannot know in detail, but at a quarter to four in the afternoon Louise Hilary was lying dead upon the floor. It is the contention of the prosecution that Charles Hilary, faced with yet another refusal to divorce him and seeing no other way out of his dilemma, wilfully and brutally murdered her."

Sir Francis allowed himself another dramatic pause.

"Having read the letter," he continued after a moment, "the police lost no time in seeking an interview with

39

Charles Hilary. Inspector Bates, the officer in charge of the investigation, asked him whether he had in fact visited Clandon Mews on the fatal day. Hilary replied with an emphatic 'No'. This was a lie—a lie which he persisted in and indeed aggravated, for he added that he had not seen his wife for several months. He stuck to his story until Inspector Bates asked him if he would be willing to have his finger-prints taken. Realising then that his lie would be exposed—for, as I have said, his finger-prints were on the bottle and the glass and, belatedly, he must have remembered handling them—he hastily changed his story. He *had* been at Clandon Mews on the day of the murder, he admitted, but not in the afternoon. He had been there, he said, for about half an hour before lunch. Members of the jury, in the submission of the prosecution we have here the classic behaviour of a man conscious of his guilt and frantically seeking to evade the consequences of his act—first, the rash lie, and then, when exposure becomes inevitable, the sudden switch to a different fiction.

"When asked to say where he did spend the afternoon, if not at Clandon Mews, Hilary declared that he had been at the Oval cricket ground, watching the Test Match between England and India. If this were true, you would think it possible that someone might have seen him and remembered him. Since his arrest, his photograph has been widely published in the newspapers and the case has been much discussed. Yet no one has come forward to say that they saw him at the Oval, or that they noticed his car parked there. Nor is it the mere lack of corroborative witnesses that throws doubt on his story. To test the truth of his statement, he was invited to describe what he could remember of the match he said he had seen, and you will hear in due course that the description he gave—which is being put in evidence—was very far from being an accurate account.

"Members of the jury, even if that were the whole of the Crown's case you would, I think, be driven irresistibly to the conclusion that Charles Hilary murdered his wife. He had motive, he had opportunity, he told a guilty lie, he failed to account convincingly for his movements at the material time. Moreover, he stands alone as a suspect—

there is no hint of any other person in this case. As I say, even if that were all it would be enough. But it is not all. Charles Hilary, who denies that he went to Clandon Mews on that Friday afternoon, was in fact seen to leave his wife's house within that period of thirty minutes during which the murder was committed. His second lie, like his first, has been exploded by the impact of irrefutable fact...."

Leo Murgatroyd, Q.C., sat tensely through the devastating opening. A short, stocky man, he was physically unimpressive, but in action he was in the top flight of defence advocates. In addition to technical skill and lucidity of mind, which were the common tools of his profession, he had those rarest of lawyer's gifts—imagination, and some understanding of human beings. On more than one occasion he had snatched a favourable verdict from seemingly certain defeat by his success in projecting a client vividly and sympathetically to a stolid jury.

Today, however, he had no confidence that such tactics would work. The prosecution's case was eighty per cent conceded—the *admitted* facts were almost enough to hang Hilary. The only hope would have been to account satisfactorily for the other twenty per cent—or at least to put forward a theory sufficiently plausible to raise a reasonable doubt. But the paucity of the defence material made that very difficult. They still knew almost nothing about Louise Hilary's activities and, as Duke had said, there was no hint of an alternative suspect.

The barrenness of the defence case was not due to any lack of effort on the part of Robert Fairey, the experienced criminal lawyer from whom Murgatroyd had received his instructions. Private detectives had been employed to investigate every aspect of Louise Hilary's life. Her immediate neighbours in the mews, who had been on holiday at the time of the murder, had been closely questioned on their return. So had Mrs. Briggs, who came in two or three times a week to clean the house. So had the tradesmen. But nothing helpful had emerged. No man had ever been seen coming to the house, or leaving it, and the char had never found any traces of a man's visit. Louise, it appeared, had spent a good deal of her time alone in the house, with her rum and her television and her magazines. When she went away she never confided to anyone where she had been or what she had been doing. She had sometimes talked to Mrs. Briggs about films she had seen, but never about her friends. Whatever secrets her life might have held, they had been skilfully kept.

One stroke of luck—or so it seemed at the time—had been the finding of several receipted hotel bills in her handbag. Agents had been sent to the seaside hotels where she had stayed, but their investigations had produced no evidence that she had spent these periods with a man. On the contrary, such information as there was suggested that she had undertaken the trips alone. Inquiries had been made, too, at several continental hotels where she had reserved a room at various times through the Wide World Agency, but the results had been the same. There had been absolutely nothing on which to build.

The solicitor's efforts to get corroboration of Hilary's own movements had been equally fruitless. No one had come forward to say they had seen him visiting the mews in the morning and, as the prosecution had pointed out, his story about going to the Oval was unsubstantiated.

In other circumstances, the position might not have worried Murgatroyd unduly, for he had had to face the same sort of thing many times before. There was often not much to be said on behalf of a guilty man, and he had defended more guilty ones than innocent. In murder cases, he knew, it was comparatively rare for an innocent man to reach the dock. Today, though, in the teeth of the evidence, he believed it had happened. The sustained and passionate indignation of Hilary and Kathryn Forrester had convinced him. What troubled him so much was that he saw no possibility of convincing anyone else. The facts, explicable and inexplicable, were overwhelming.

The first few witnesses had only routine evidence to give, and the coughing and shuffling of feet in court marked the release of tension. A surveyor proved a plan of the house at Clandon Mews and a police photographer the pictures he had taken of the scene. The messenger boy described his discovery of the body, and evidence was called confirming the time of the 999 call.

Next came William Harbin, the wide-awake young clerk from the travel agency. He explained that Mrs. Hilary had ordered a single ticket to Paris at twenty-four hours' notice and had rung up to make certain it had been secured. He knew her voice well and was in no doubt about her identity. He could swear to the time because he had looked at the clock when she had asked him about the ticket.

When Sir Francis had finished with Harbin, Murgatroyd put a few questions.

"Did Mrs. Hilary happen to mention the purpose of her visit to the Continent?"

"She said she was going on holiday."

"Did she say why she wanted only a single ticket?"

"I gathered she hadn't made any definite plans. She said she wasn't sure where she would be going to after Paris and might come back another way."

"Was that her habit—to go away without definite plans?"

"No, she usually went to one special place."

"And took a return ticket?"

"Yes."

"Was it customary for her to give such short notice?"

"No, she generally told us well in advance."

Sir Francis gave the faintest shrug as Murgatroyd sat down, and called his next witness, the pathologist who had conducted the post-mortem. After a brief examination Murgatroyd again intervened and got the doctor to say that in his opinion Louise Hilary had been under the influence of alcohol at the time of her death, that there were indications of her having been a regular heavy drinker and heavy smoker and a mild drug taker, and that the state of the body suggested that in general she had followed a far from healthy mode of life. This time the judge looked puzzled too, but he made no comment.

Next came Detective-Inspector Warren, one of the Yard's finger-print experts. He described how he had gone over the house in Clandon Mews for prints and had found identifiable ones of only three people—Louise Hilary herself, Mrs. Briggs and the prisoner. Murgatroyd did his best with this awkward piece of evidence.

"Did you find the prisoner's finger-prints anywhere

else in the house except on the bottle and on the tumbler?"

"No."

"So although, as he himself agrees, he was in the house for some time, he would have left no trace of his visit if he hadn't happened to touch those objects?"

"That is so."

"Then it's reasonable to suppose, isn't it, that if some other man had visited the house and stayed there for a while and not happened to touch those objects, he also might have left no prints?"

"I suppose so."

"A criminal doesn't always leave finger-prints?"

"Oh, no."

"Speaking as an expert, Inspector, is it your experience that criminals are rather conscious these days of the danger of leaving their finger-prints behind?"

"Unfortunately, yes."

"Men who have made up their minds to commit a crime often take precautions against leaving finger-prints, or at least exercise great care?"

"That is so."

"Whereas an innocent man, of course, wouldn't bother about it?"

"No."

"Thank you."

Inspector Bates followed. He described the scene at the house when he arrived and his discovery of the letter and gave evidence about the absence of clues pointing to anyone but Hilary. Sir Francis took him carefully through his first interview with the prisoner, and the interrogation at the police station, and the circumstances leading to the arrest.

Once again Murgatroyd's questions caused some surprise. He was interested in the state of the house—the unmade bed, the rum stains on the television set, the general appearance of untidiness and neglect. Apart from that, he managed to extract one helpful admission—that the prisoner had shown surprise and horror on being told the news about his wife. The inspector succeeded in conveying by his manner, however, that he personally had not been taken in by it.

44

After Bates came a silver-haired, pink-faced man who took the oath in a pleasant, cultured voice. He was examined by Forbes, Sir Francis's junior.

"Is your name Henry George Salcombe and do you live at 38A Manor Road, Barnet?"

"Yes."

"Are you a professional sports commentator?"

"I am."

"Have you made a special study of the game of cricket and have you played for your county and have you written three books on the subject?"

"Yes."

"Were you at the Oval cricket ground on the afternoon of Friday, June 3rd?"

"Yes."

"Were you giving the commentary that afternoon for the B.B.C.'s television service?"

"I was."

"Now, Mr. Salcombe, you have heard read out in court the series of questions about this match which were put to the prisoner by Inspector Bates on June 4th and the prisoner's answers?"

"Yes."

"Had you previously had an opportunity of studying these questions and answers?"

"Yes."

"Was the prisoner's account of what happened at the match an accurate one?"

"It was very inaccurate. There were two mistakes in describing how batsmen got out—one man was described as having been caught out instead of run out, and the other as bowled instead of l.b.w. On three occasions the wrong fieldsman was referred to, and on two occasions the wrong bowler. Two errors were also made about the state of the score."

"Thank you."

"No questions," growled Murgatroyd. Hilary had been altogether too wide of the mark to make bickering about details worth while. If only, he thought, his client had had the sense to seek advice before plunging into that gratuitous description! He would do his best to explain the errors away when the time came, but he wasn't at all sure that he

45

would succeed. He noticed two of the jurymen exchanging meaning glances, and wondered how many of the ten men were cricket fans.

Sir Francis rose portentously. "I call Mary Agnes Scott."

The court, which had taken a lively interest in the evidence of the celebrated Henry Salcombe, became very still again as the new witness took the oath. The woman's kindly face was even more worried-looking than when Charles had seen her at the identification parade.

"Is your name Mary Agnes Scott?"

"Yes."

"Are you forty-one years of age, a housewife, married, with three children, and do you live at 14 Everton Road, Kensington?"

"Yes."

"Is your husband a schoolmaster employed by the London County Council?"

"Yes."

"Mrs. Scott, did you on the afternoon of Friday, June 3rd, walk past the end of Clandon Mews?"

"Yes."

"At about what time?"

"It was nearly half past three."

"Can you say that with certainty?"

"Yes, I looked at the clock just before I left home. I was going to pick up some ointment at Swallow's, the chemist's, and it was to be ready at half past three."

"Was your clock about right, do you know?"

"It was a minute or two fast."

"Very well. Now, Mrs. Scott, will you tell the court what you saw as you passed the end of Clandon Mews?"

"I saw a man coming out of the first flat, the one nearest the road."

"Did you call at your local police station on the following morning and say that you had seen this man?"

"Yes."

"What made you do that?"

"Well, I read in the newspaper that a woman had been found murdered at 1 Clandon Mews and that the police wanted to talk to anyone who had seen anybody around there that afternoon. I went along to the mews to see if Number 1 was the house I had seen the man coming out of, and it was, so I thought I ought to tell the police."

"You were acting from a sense of public duty?"

"Yes, it seemed the right thing to do."

"Quite so—I am sure the court will agree that you acted very properly. Did you give a description of the man to the police that morning?"

"I tried to, yes."

"How did you describe him?"

"I said that he was tall and very sunburned and that he wasn't wearing a hat and that I thought he had brown hair."

"Were you prompted or questioned while you were giving this description, or did you say it straight out like that?"

"I said it straight out."

"Were you subsequently taken by Inspector Johnson to Gate Street police station to see if you could identify the man?"

"Yes."

"Was there any discussion on the way about your description or about any person who might answer to it?"

"No."

"What happened when you got to Gate Street police station?"

"I sat in a little room for a few minutes and then I was taken into a yard where there were a lot of men in a row, and another policeman, Inspector Bates, said 'Can you see the man here?'"

"And could you?"

"Yes, I picked him out at once."

"You had no difficulty?"

"None at all."

"Were you quite certain that the man you picked out was the man you saw coming out of 1 Clandon Mews at about half past three on the previous afternoon?"

"Yes."

"Are you still quite certain?"

"Yes."

47

"To the best of your knowledge, had you ever seen this man prior to that occasion?"

"No."

"Can you see the man in court now?"

"Yes."

"Please point him out."

"That's the man—the prisoner."

Murgatroyd rose unhurriedly, and for a moment regarded the woman, whose evidence, unless he was very much mistaken, was going to hang his client. He had studied her demeanour in the magistrate's court and had been favourably impressed by her manner. She was just the sort of witness to have a big effect upon a jury and he knew that unless he handled her very carefully indeed he might do more harm than good.

"Mrs. Scott, you do realise, I am sure, that a man's life may depend upon the evidence you are giving?"

"Yes, I realise that."

"So that if there is the least doubt in your mind, the merest shadow of a doubt, you should say so."

"I would, I really would, but there isn't."

"Very well. Now how long have you lived at 14 Everton Road?"

"About five years."

"So you know the neighbourhood quite well?"

"Yes."

"You get about quite a bit—shopping, that sort of thing?"

"Yes."

"I expect you have often passed the end of Clandon Mews?"

"Oh, very often."

"You say that on this Friday afternoon you were going to the chemist's to pick up some ointment. What was the ointment for?"

"My little boy had developed a skin rash on his face."

"Yes, I see. A nasty rash?"

"It was very unsightly."

"So you were naturally anxious to get the ointment as soon as possible?"

"Yes."

48

"In that case, I don't suppose you loitered on your way to the chemist's?"

"Oh, no, I didn't loiter."

"You walked rather fast?"

"Well, not fast—it was a hot day."

"A good steady pace?"

"Yes."

"What made you look into Clandon Mews as you passed by?"

"I heard a noise—I think it must have been the door of the house being slammed."

"So you turned your head, and you saw a man?"

"Yes."

"About how far from you would you say he was when you saw him?"

"I should think about—well, five or six yards."

"Was he near the door?"

"He was just moving away from it."

"In what direction was he looking?"

"He was looking towards me."

"Mrs. Scott, as you walked past the end of the mews and saw this man, did you stop?"

"Oh, no."

"Did you check your pace?"

"No."

"You heard the noise and just glanced round at him as you passed?"

"Yes."

"If you only gave him a passing glance, you couldn't of course have *studied* his face?"

"No, I didn't study it."

"Did you think anything about the incident at the time?"

"No, not at the time."

"There was nothing about it that made it particularly noteworthy?"

"No."

"Did you, for instance, think to yourself at the time 'that's a strange-looking man', or 'that's a handsome man', or 'that's a worried-looking man'—anything like that?"

"No."

"Did you notice his clothes?"

"No."

"That description you gave to the police—'tall, sun-burned, bare-headed, brown hair'—it could apply to a lot of people, couldn't it?"

"Yes."

"Did you make any attempt to describe his features?"

"No."

"Was that because you'd received no more than an impression?"

"Yes, but it was a very clear impression. I couldn't describe his face but I knew it at once directly I saw it again."

"I appreciate that, but it is a fact, isn't it, that you couldn't remember any details of it—any particular details about the eyes or nose or mouth, for instance?"

"Nothing particular, no—just the face in general."

"So that when you attended the identification parade you weren't looking for a man with any particular facial characteristics that you'd made a mental note of at the time?"

"No, I was just seeing if I could recognise the face I'd seen."

"A face of which you had received a passing impression on a single occasion."

"Yes."

Murgatroyd glanced at the jury and sat down with every appearance of contentment. For a moment, as prosecuting counsel conferred together, he thought that they were going to re-examine, but Sir Francis seemed satisfied and proceeded to call his last witness, the police officer who had made the arrangements for the identification parade. This man explained how the volunteers had been obtained and described the precautions that had been taken to make the parade a fair one. Hilary, he pointed out, had been allowed to choose his own position in the line and care had been taken to see that Mrs. Scott did not catch a glimpse of him on his own before she was led into the yard.

"No questions," said Murgatroyd.

Sir Francis folded up his notes, and half-rose. "That, my Lord, completes the case for the Crown."

"Then I think," said Mr. Justice Green, who had hardly spoken a word all morning, "that this might be a convenient moment to adjourn for lunch." He got up and bowed and slipped away, and at once a babel of talk broke the silence.   Kathryn gave Charles an encouraging wave as he was taken below, but her smile was fleeting.   If she hadn't known it herself, she could have seen from Murgatroyd's grim expression that things were not going well. She took her brother's arm and went out past the waiting battery of cameras.   As the police shepherded her through the crowd, some women hissed her.

CHAPTER V

"My Lord, I call the prisoner."

With his police escort close behind him, Charles stepped from the dock and made his way across the small, intimate court-room to the witness-box. He knew that necks were craning from the gallery; he could sense the heightened air of expectancy that marked the descent of the star performer into the arena. He had feared the ordeal of this moment—feared that he might show in some outward and humiliating way, by some stumble or some hesitancy, the strain he was going through. In fact, though, as he moved towards the box he grew more composed, more sure of himself, than he had been at any time since the opening of the trial. There was something sustaining, he found, about the blaze of limelight now turned full upon him and the knowledge that he had the stage to himself. A vain man might even find pleasure, however transient, in being the target and focus of all eyes while the deadly personal battle was on. He wasn't vain, but he was proud, and he hated the submissive silence of the dock. At least he could defend himself now as man to man, and it would be less humbling to the ego to be talked *to* than talked about. No doubt it was absurdly sensitive of him to resent being referred to as "Hilary" and "the prisoner" when they were going to hang him anyway, but that was how he felt.

"Take the book in your right hand," said the clerk. "Repeat after me . . ."

Murgatroyd had given long and anxious thought to the defence strategy before finally deciding that he must put his client into the witness-box. The dangers of doing so were, he knew, very great. In this case, the only defence was a denial, and you couldn't prove a negative. Whatever Hilary said, he couldn't hope to disprove the prosecution's charge, and he would be subjected to a cross-examination that might well be lethal. If the Crown's case had been less strong, Murgatroyd would have called no evidence and stood pat upon "He didn't do it, he wasn't there, he knows nothing whatever about it—now convince the jury beyond a shadow of doubt". But as things were, he dared not do that. If Hilary didn't go into the box he would indubitably be convicted. The only hope was that the prisoner's personality under questioning would more than counterbalance the evidence in the minds of the jury. It was a slender hope, but Murgatroyd had known such things to happen.

The initial impression, at least, was good. Hilary neither looked nor sounded like a guilty man as he stood upright with one hand on the ledge in front of him and quietly took the oath. Seven weeks of mental stress had hollowed his cheeks and thinned his face and given him a rather fine, ascetic appearance. No one, seeing him now, could readily believe him capable of violence and brutal passion.

Murgatroyd turned squarely upon him.

"Charles Hilary, did you murder your wife?"

"I did not."

The impact of the direct question and the equally direct answer, coming unexpectedly at the very beginning of the examination, was dramatic. The defence had got away to a clean start. In his very brief opening remarks Murgatroyd had declared that Hilary had nothing whatever to hide, and now he would try to justify his claim.

He proceeded on a more conversational note, putting his questions unhurriedly and giving the jury plenty of time to digest the answers. It was of vital importance to slow down the racing tempo of this trial. The prosecution, perhaps without intending to, had managed to leave the impression on the court that all was over bar the verdict. Murgatroyd might lose his case in the end, but he certainly wasn't going to have his client hustled off to the gallows like that. He intended that the jury should get to know Hilary; that they should see as much of him as possible.

Step by step, Charles was guided through his long and not unmoving story. Everything was faithfully dealt with —his twenty years of distinguished service in the West Indies, the nature of his work, how he had come to meet

Louise, the failure of the marriage, and the causes of the eventual separation. He told how he had installed her in the house in Clandon Mews; he told of his meeting with Kathryn, and his visits and letters to Louise asking for a divorce, and the gathering crisis in his relations with Kathryn culminating on the evening before the murder when she had said they must live together or part. So far it was the prosecution's case, admitted and expanded, but now came the first denial.

"Mr. Hilary, when Miss Forrester suggested on the night before the murder that you and she should go away and live together openly, what was your attitude?"

"I was very much opposed to it."

"Why?"

"I wasn't convinced that I could make her happy in those conditions and I hated the idea of her having to give up her job on account of me. She'd achieved so much, and I was proud of her."

"When you say that you were opposed to her suggestion, do you mean that you had decided against it?"

"No, I hadn't decided anything definitely at that time. I told Kathryn—Miss Forrester—that I would make one more approach to my wife and that if she was still adamant we'd talk about it again."

"The matter was still open?"

"Certainly."

"You have heard the submission of the prosecution that at the time you visited your wife you were faced with a choice between getting rid of her or losing Miss Forrester?"

"I have, but that wasn't the situation at all. Although we had a difference of opinion—Miss Forrester and I— there was never any real question of our breaking things up. Miss Forrester wanted us to go away, and I knew that in the last resort that was probably what we should do."

"Did you in fact come to a decision when you saw her again on the Friday evening?"

"Yes, we talked about it again and we finally agreed that she should give up her job and that we would go to France and look for a place to live."

"If you had already killed your wife, that decision would have been superfluous, would it not?"

"Completely."

"Did you at any time consider killing your wife as a way out of your difficulty?"

"Not for an instant. It wasn't a thing that would ever have occurred to me."

"Apart from any question of right or wrong, can you imagine that it could ever have been a solution of your problem?"

"In no circumstances. It would have been madness. If I'd done a thing like that I'd have had it on my mind for the rest of my life. Everything would have been ruined."

"The most irregular union would have been preferable?"

"Infinitely."

"Mr. Hilary, after you and Miss Forrester had taken this decision to go away together, what did you do? I mean later that evening?"

"We went out to celebrate."

"What form did the celebration take?"

"We dined out at a restaurant and had a bottle of champagne and then we danced a little."

"You *danced*?"

"Yes."

Murgatroyd gave a satisfied nod. He knew that the line he was taking might strike some of the pundits as foolhardy, but as he had already made up his mind that the defence had nothing whatever to lose, shock tactics seemed justified.

He reverted now to the actual interview between Charles and Louise. Here again, the utmost candour seemed called for, since Hilary had already told the police almost everything in his original statement and further admissions were the best way of inoculating the jury against the conclusions which the prosecution would undoubtedly draw. The scene at Clandon Mews was therefore reconstructed in graphic detail, and, because the picture was true in every particular, with great impressiveness. Finally, Murgatroyd touched on a specific matter which he knew he had to bring out.

"Mr. Hilary, did you ever consider the possibility that you might some day be able to start divorce proceedings yourself?"

"It had occurred to me."

"At this interview with your wife, after she had again refused your request, did you mention the possibility?"

"I did."

"What did she say?"

"She laughed and said she was much too discreet and that I'd never get any evidence."

"Did she deny that there were any grounds?"

"No. I rather gathered that she was having affairs but that she was determined not to let them be known about. She said she hated me and was going to make sure I was tied to her for ever."

"And that was why she was being so secretive?"

"That was what I gathered."

"Since your separation, did you at any time see her in company with a man?"

"I saw her one lunch-time getting into a taxi with someone in Piccadilly."

"So she did have men friends?"

"Evidently."

Again Murgatroyd nodded, but this time his satisfaction was assumed. It had been necessary to bring up the matter in this way, for no one else could say anything about Louise Hilary's private life. Nevertheless, he had no illusions about the probable consequences. He could almost hear prosecuting counsel sharpening his knife.

Item by item, as the examination continued, all the main points in the Crown's case were dealt with. Charles described his movements after leaving his wife, and the state of mind he was in. Now that he had admitted his momentary impulse to do violence to Louise, he was able to explain more convincingly both the cause of his preoccupation at the Oval and the reasons which had later led him to lie to the police.

There was nothing left now but the last formal denials.

"You have heard the testimony of Mrs. Scott that she saw you leaving your wife's house that afternoon?"

"She is mistaken. I wasn't there."

"You were at the Oval?"

"Yes."

"You swear that on your oath?"

"I do."

"Charles Hilary, I ask you again—had you anything to do with your wife's death?"

"Nothing whatever. I am absolutely innocent."

Murgatroyd gave the jury a challenging look, and resumed his seat. Charles braced himself to meet the prosecuting counsel's onslaught.

In fact, the cross-examination proved to be less gruelling than he had expected. So much was now admitted by the defence that there was little further advance to be made by the prosecution. Sir Francis probed a little deeper into the motives which had led to the disastrous lie and dwelt for a while on the angry scene with Louise, but Charles was on the unshakable ground of truth and simply adhered to his story. It was only when Duke turned to the defence's attempt to conjure up an alternative suspect that matters became difficult.

"Mr. Hilary, you have told us that you once saw your wife getting into a taxi with a man—I believe you said at lunch-time. Can you describe this man?"

"No, I only caught a glimpse of his back."

"Have you any idea at all who he was?"

"None."

"Just a man?"

"Yes."

"Are you suggesting that getting into a taxi with a man at lunch-time—I am assuming for the moment that you haven't invented the whole episode—is evidence of adultery?"

"Of course not."

"But you did suggest, did you not, that your wife had had immoral relations with other men?"

"I said she practically admitted having affairs."

"Please don't quibble. Are you or are you not asserting that in your view she had immoral relations with other men?"

"I suppose so, yes, if you want to call them immoral."

"What would you call them?"

"I'm hardly in a position to call them anything."

"That is certainly true. Mr. Hilary, have you any idea who these hypothetical men friends were?"

"None. I've had almost nothing to do with my wife for two years—I know almost nothing about her life."

"Yet you accuse her of infidelity. Have you in fact a scrap of evidence that she was ever unfaithful to you?"

"Only the evidence of her own attitude."

"Did you ever know her to be unfaithful to you during your years together in the West Indies?"

"Much of the time I had little idea what she was doing. I was away a great deal."

"Answer my question. Did you ever know?"

"No."

"And since your return to England have you any positive evidence that she was ever unfaithful to you?"

"No."

"In fact, you are trying to blacken your dead wife's character without a single shred of proof?"

Charles flushed angrily. How had he ever got into this position? Of course Louise had had men friends—she'd always been highly sexed and it was inconceivable that she'd lived a celibate life all these years, and besides, she *had* virtually admitted it."

"Well, Mr. Hilary?"

"I don't want to blacken her character—I don't even think she'd have regarded it that way herself. I'm simply telling you what I believe are the facts."

"Did you ever take any steps to test your belief? You wanted a divorce very badly—did you think of employing a private inquiry agent?"

"I thought of it, but I decided against it."

"Why?"

"For various reasons. The idea of spying wasn't very attractive and in any case I wasn't at all sure that I should succeed in an action. Besides, I hadn't lost hope that she would divorce me."

"I put it to you that the reason you took no action was because you didn't really believe there was anything to find out?"

"That isn't so."

"I put it to you that this story of yours about the infidelity of your wife and about seeing her with a man in a taxi is a complete fabrication from start to finish. I submit that the whole purpose of your evidence has been to deflect suspicion from yourself on to some entirely non-existent lover?"

"I don't think he is non-existent. I didn't kill her, so there must have been someone else."

Sir Francis looked grim.

"That will be for the jury to decide."

Kathryn was silent as John Forrester drove her home after the adjournment. She had great faith in Murgatroyd, and perhaps things would look different after he had made his final speech, but so far it seemed to her that there had been almost no defence at all. If only they could have *proved* something and not just had to rely on unsupported suggestion about Louise! Everybody said that Fairey was a very astute lawyer and presumably his inquiries had covered all the ground, but she couldn't help wishing that he had taken her more into his confidence. She would have been only too glad to try to get some evidence herself, but he had made it plain from the start that he thought the less she had to do with the case the better, and her offer of help had been rather stiffly turned down.

She had begged to be allowed to give evidence in court, but the lawyers had finally decided against that too, and Charles had strongly supported them. She could see Murgatroyd's point, of course—although she was the only person who could corroborate any part of Charles's testimony, she was also a very interested party, and anything she had said would have been heavily discounted. It might even have strengthened public doubts about her own share in the affair, which was the thing that had weighed most with Charles. Murgatroyd had agreed that she might have made a good personal impression on the court, but he had also feared that the impression might be too good, and the jury might decide she was the sort of woman a man might kill for. Was it sensible, he had asked, to flaunt the prize? Kathryn still wasn't convinced. Mightn't they think it strange, even sinister, that she hadn't gone into the box to back her lover up?

Still, the decision had been taken and it was unlikely that Murgatroyd would change his mind now. Perhaps it *had* been better to leave it all to Charles—his very isolation must have won him some sympathy. He had done very well—his answers to Murgatroyd had been careful and thoughtful, with nothing evasive about them, and nothing theatrical. Of course, he had been indignant with that horrible man Duke, but it had been honest indignation and

59

couldn't have done any harm.   It was surely impossible that any jury could have doubted he was telling the truth? —they must have realised that he was an innocent man caught in a net.   Tomorrow they would say so.   It was unthinkable that they could do anything else. . . .

There were no oratorical flourishes about Sir Francis's closing speech next morning.

"The Crown," he said, "seeks no victory, but only justice based on facts.   If the facts fail to convince you, members of the jury, if there remains the slightest element of reasonable doubt in your minds, then it will be your duty and I am sure your pleasure to find in favour of the prisoner.   Now let me recapitulate those facts. . . ."

With cold, impersonal detachment, he proceeded to recall the points on which the prosecution relied—the prisoner's desperate predicament, the angry interview, the guilty lie, the creaking alibi, the proved identification.

"The prisoner has said that when he went to see his wife that day he had no cause to kill her, since it was open to him to solve his problem by going away and living with his mistress.   That may be so.   But the question you have to decide, ladies and gentlemen, is whether that thought was in his mind at the time of the interview.   He has admitted his extreme reluctance to take such a step.   There was certainly no indication in his letter that it was in his mind —rather the reverse, for you will remember that he spoke of an 'impasse', a dead end.   Is it not likely—is it not certain, in the light of all the evidence—that when that angry interview was at its height he thought of nothing but the obstacle in his path, and in the fury of the moment removed it once and for all?

"You have heard his explanation of the lie he told the police.   He says that, though innocent, he felt in danger. You will have to ask yourselves whether that is the natural reaction of an innocent man, particularly of a man who claims to have believed that his wife had secret lovers. Would you not have expected him to wonder *who* might have done this thing, rather than to assume that on the strength of a single letter he had written, and because of an impulse which he declares he resisted, he himself must be blamed?

"As for those mythical lovers, it will not have escaped you that the defence has brought no jot of evidence to prove their existence. All it has done is to throw up a smokescreen of suggestion. It is true now, as it was when this case opened, that Hilary stands alone as a suspect.

"You may think that, on the whole, the prisoner acquitted himself well in the witness-box. But the prisoner is a highly intelligent man, and a skilful front of innocence must not be confused with innocence itself. Hilary would not be the first murderer to show consummate artistry in the box. You will, of course, have formed your own judgment; but in the last resort it is the facts which must decide.

"The identification of the prisoner by Mrs. Scott has been challenged, but in no way weakened. At no time did she make any exaggerated statement; at no time did she have to retract anything she had said. She volunteered her description of a man, at the earliest opportunity and without any persuasion or assistance, solely from her recollection of him, and that description, though vague, tallied with the appearance of the prisoner. She made no attempt to describe more than she had seen; she admitted frankly that she had gained only a passing impression of a face. But the briefest impression of a face can stay clearly in the mind, as an instantaneous exposure can stay clearly on a photographic plate. That it did so is shown by what followed. Without having seen the prisoner before, except on that one occasion when he was leaving the house—without having had him described to her or having seen a picture of him, she picked him out at once from a choice of twelve. This, in the submission of the prosecution, is an identification to which the very greatest weight must be attached.

"Members of the jury, no consideration of sentiment or sympathy must deter you from doing your duty. If you have any doubt that Charles Hilary strangled his wife, he must be freed. But if you come to the conclusion that, driven on by guilty passion, he sent her to her account, then it is your inescapable duty to send Hilary to his account.

As he sat down, Kathryn looked at Charles. This time she could not force a smile. Her face had a look of frozen horror.

•　　•　　•　　•　　•

"May it please your Lordship."

Murgatroyd rose for the last time and turned to face the double row of worried men and women to whose intelligence and sensibility he was now to make his final appeal.

"Members of the jury, I am not going to pretend that the prosecution has not brought a very powerful case against the prisoner, or that the task of defence has been easy. This is no ordinary case that you are trying, where evidence can be weighed against evidence. Charles Hilary stands in danger of his life for a crime of which he is so innocent, indeed so ignorant, that it is hard to know where to seek a reply. It can rarely have happened that circumstances have so conspired against a man.

"By far the most damaging piece of evidence brought against the prisoner is, of course, that of identification offered by Mrs. Scott. Let me say at once that her good faith is not, and never has been, in question. We accept that she did see a man leaving Clandon Mews at half past three on June 3rd, and that in general appearance he was not unlike the prisoner, and that she genuinely believes him to have been the prisoner. We accept that this man was in all probability the murderer of Louise Hilary. But we deny that he was Charles Hilary—we say that Mrs. Scott has made a mistake. Now how could such an honest but calamitous mistake have come about?

"All I can do, members of the jury, is to offer you a theory, but it is a theory so easily credible that it can hardly fail to raise a doubt in your minds. Let us go back for a moment to the substance of Mrs. Scott's testimony. She took with her to Gate Street police station, you will remember, the impression of a face which had resulted from a passing glance. She knew that she was being asked to pick out, if she could, the face of a man she had seen on one occasion. She was looking, in fact, for a *familiar* face out of those twelve lined up—a familiar face associated in her mind with a man leaving Clandon Mews.

"Now bear this in mind—Charles Hilary was not entirely a stranger to Clandon Mews. He had been there on several occasions prior to that Friday—first, when the house was being furnished, and later to plead personally with his wife for a divorce. Mrs. Scott herself was a frequent passer-by, for the mews lay on her everyday route to the shops. She has told us that to the best of her knowledge she had not set eyes on Hilary before June 3rd, but is it not conceivable that this is the source of her mistake? All of you must agree that it is easier to remember the outlines of a face than to remember the exact occasion on which it was seen. Is it not conceivable that in fact it was on one of those *earlier* occasions that Mrs. Scott passed the end of the mews and saw Charles Hilary as he was leaving the house?

"If that be so, what took place at the identification parade is no longer damning evidence against Hilary. Mrs. Scott, I repeat, was looking for a face associated in her mind with a man leaving Clandon Mews, and with nothing else. If the murderer was not among those twelve, but Hilary was, would she not inevitably have picked him out? The familiar face, seen once and in similar circumstances, and in general characteristics not unlike the murderer's own ...? I suggest to you that this is precisely what happened.

"Members of the jury, I cannot stress too strongly the uncertainties and dangers of this kind of identification from memory. The records of our courts contain example after example of positive identifications made in good faith which subsequently proved to be wrong. Oscar Slater spent the best years of his life breaking stones in the quarries of Peterhead after numerous witnesses had identified him as a man suspected of murdering an old lady, yet it is now recognised that he was innocent and the witnesses mistaken. Adolf Beck was positively identified as a criminal by ten or a dozen different women, yet in the end it was conclusively proved that he was not the man at all. How much more reluctant, then, should we be to accept the present identification by a single witness, and on the strength of it consign the prisoner to a fate which is final and irremediable?"

Murgatroyd paused to satisfy himself that he had the jury's close attention and finding that he had, pressed on.

"Ladies and gentlemen, once the value of this identification is seen in its true perspective, the whole case against Hilary takes on a very different aspect. What are we left with?

"A motive, says the Crown—he had to kill his wife to keep his mistress. Well, you have heard the prisoner's own

63

comment on that supposed dilemma, and his emphatic statement that another course lay open to him. That alternative, little though he liked it—and about that, as about all other matters in this case, he has been very frank— was unquestionably an easier and safer and altogether more hopeful one than murder. A man might well be reluctant to see a woman sacrifice a fine career on his account and even more reluctant to ask her to 'live in sin' with him, as the saying goes; but a man would have to be a mental as well as a moral defective who chose killing in preference. Whatever the immediate problems and difficulties which lay in the path of these lovers, they must have known that time was surely on their side and that in the end their difficulties would pass.

"What else are we left with? A lie, says the Crown—a lie that proves guilt. Members of the jury, it is easy to be high-minded in a court of law, and to forget our common weaknesses when we sit in judgment. But the fact is that a man does not have to be a murderer because he tells a lie, nor even wicked. That lie to the police was most regrettable and most improper, but it can well bear the explanation which Hilary put on it. Is it only the guilty who are permitted an instinct of self-preservation? Hilary saw, and saw clearly, that a web of circumstantial evidence might close around him, and the very situation in which he now finds himself is proof that his innocent fears were justified.

"What else, again? An unlikely alibi, says the prosecution, which cannot be proved. That is true—we cannot prove it, nor can we prove that the prisoner visited his wife between twelve-thirty and one o'clock. But is it really surprising that no witnesses have appeared to corroborate Hilary's account of his movements? He is not a particularly unusual or striking-looking man. He has no obvious deformities, no long black beard—nothing, at a casual glance, to distinguish him outwardly from the mass of his fellows. Is it then beyond belief that he should be able to pay a brief visit to a mews without people coming forward afterwards to say they saw him? Is it beyond belief that he should not have been noticed at the Oval? There were thousands, tens of thousands, of people on the cricket ground, and no doubt all but Hilary himself were concentrating on the match they had paid to see. Why should anyone have remembered him? As for the inaccuracy of his recollections, he has accounted for that, and his reason is valid. On that matter I will say only this—that if Hilary had really not been at the Oval that day, he would hardly have acceded to the police request that he should describe what he had seen. The mere attempt was an indication of clear conscience, if not of clear memory.

"So what has become of the prosecution case, which is supposed to leave you in no doubt? We have not disproved it, but we have answered it. We have answered every single point, and reasonably.

"Let me now turn to the psychological improbabilities of the Crown's case. You have seen Charles Hilary in the dock and in the witness-box, and have doubtless formed your own view of him. You have heard about his work, his interests, his activities. You have studied his demeanour. He is a quiet, reflective man; a man who thinks before he talks or acts. His life has been devoted to research, to the improvement of agriculture, to the betterment of the lot of his fellows. His ways have always been civilised and kindly.

"Now think for a moment what this man is alleged to have done. If the prosecution is right, he slew his wife by choking the life out of her with his bare hands. Then, without a trace of pity or regret, he went straightaway to his mistress and took her out to celebrate—to dine and drink champagne and *dance*! If Charles Hilary did that, with his wife's murder fresh on his conscience and the feel of her neck in his fingers, then he is as cold-blooded and heartless a monster as has ever appeared before our criminal courts. But, members of the jury, look at him! Do you see him as a monster? Or do you see him as he is?—a gentle and innocent man, in mortal peril of a wrong judgment?

"Finally, I wish to touch briefly on another aspect of this case. It is not, of course, the task of the defence to produce an alternative suspect, nor can we do so. But consider the facts. Louise Hilary was not a very pleasant person. She had separated from her husband by mutual agreement and was being kept by him in comfort, even in luxury. She did not love him—she did not even like him. She hated him, this man on whose generosity she was content to live. Knowing his predicament and the fearful harm she was doing to him, she refused to divorce him. You may say she had the right to take that stand and the legal right she undoubtedly had, but by any ordinary human standards her action was vindictive and venomous. What else do we know about her? She was a confirmed and habitual drunkard, almost a dipsomaniac. She drugged herself to sleep, and she drugged herself awake. In the home she was a slattern—the bed unmade at three in the afternoon, the costly carpet burned with cigarettes, the marks of bottles on the polished furniture. Would I be exaggerating if I said that the picture which emerges is that of a self-indulgent, heartless and neurotic slut? I think not.

"Yet she was not without some physical attraction—you have seen her photograph. She had been very pretty, and though her way of life had played havoc with her looks, she was far from being devoid of any physical appeal. Is it straining credulity too far to suggest the possibility—more, the likelihood—that such a woman would have a lover, or lovers? You may say we have produced no evidence, and that is true. But this woman, remember, had an almost pathological determination to thwart her husband and deny him happiness. She blamed him for her own failures, and this was her morbidly-conceived revenge. To prevent Hilary becoming free, she was prepared to go to extreme lengths of concealment about her own private life. I leave this question in your minds—did Louise Hilary have lovers, and if she did, is it not possible that one of them might have killed her? Can you reasonably rule it out?

"We know that she was about to leave the country at twenty-four hours' notice and without definite plans, a thing she had never done before. What impelled her to take that sudden and unprecedented step? Can we be certain that it was unconnected with the crime that was so soon to take place? The fact is that we know almost nothing about this woman's life during the past two years, and that very gap in our knowledge should give us pause. Is it safe to convict the prisoner against a background of such abysmal ignorance? Can you honestly feel that you have heard the whole truth?

"Members of the jury, there is a doubt, and where there is a doubt—as my learned friend has told you—your duty is plain. Only by a verdict of 'Not Guilty' can you make certain of avoiding that most fearful of possibilities—a miscarriage of justice on a capital charge."

As Murgatroyd had developed his warming, confident appeal, the icy lump at Kathryn's heart had begun to thaw. It was going to be all right after all—she ought never to have doubted. It was only that the prosecuting counsel had somehow managed to make the case sound so much stronger than it really was—but now it was in tatters. Why, there was really no case at all. Murgatroyd had been splendid, he'd made everything so clear. What he had said about Charles was absolutely right and the jury was bound to see it. A monster!—how preposterous! And that explanation of his about Mrs. Scott's identification had been brilliant—it was obviously just what had happened. The trial would soon be over now—just the summing-up, and after that the jury shouldn't need long for their verdict. Charles would soon be free again, and she'd be able to take him away and look after him and they'd try to forget it all. . . .

But as Kathryn listened to the judge's summing-up, fear crept back. In a few moments, the whole atmosphere of the court had changed again, and all the good effects of Murgatroyd's electrifying speech seemed to have been lost. With his platitudes and his qualifications, the judge was spreading a cloak of greyness over everything. Worse still, he was going back over all that dreary evidence. . . .

"You will have to decide, members of the jury, whether or not you accept Mrs. Scott's evidence of identification as reliable. The defence say that she was mistaken and have put forward a theory which they claim might account for such a mistake. You may or may not think that that theory is a reasonable one—that is entirely a matter for you. The possibility of error based on a fleeting personal impression is a very real one, and you will bear that in mind. At the same time, you should not allow yourselves to be swayed by references to mistakes in identifications in earlier trials where the circumstances were entirely different. You are considering the evidence of Mrs. Scott on its merits. If you feel any doubt about her identification, any doubt whatever, then you must consider very seriously whether the rest of the prosecution's evidence is conclusive. If on the other hand you accept her evidence that Hilary was at the house that afternoon, then you can hardly fail to come to the conclusion that he is guilty."

Point by point, the judge went over the well-worn ground with well-worn phrases. Sometimes he seemed to lean a little to one side, sometimes a little to the other, but always he regained his middle position, like a toy on leaden feet. On the question of motive, for instance—"the defence have said that Hilary knew he had a better way out than murder during that interview with his wife, but you may well feel that a man may not necessarily remember the better way out when he is engaged in a furious scene with someone who is an obstacle to his plans." Or on the subject of Hilary's description of the cricket match— "You may well be impressed with the defence's submission that a man who had not been near a cricket ground would be unlikely readily to submit himself to a detailed interrogation about what had happened during the game."

So it went on, with much reading of evidence and reiteration of arguments, until even the jury began to stir restlessly. Everything was mentioned, but nothing was really illuminated. There was the usual instruction that the prisoner was not required to prove his innocence; the usual reminder that the court was not a court of morals; the usual advice about what constituted "reasonable doubt".

"You must not say to yourselves, 'We don't know much about Louise Hilary and it's always possible that any one of dozens of people might have wanted to kill her'—that is not reasonable doubt. Nor must you say to yourselves, 'We have seen Hilary in the witness-box and he seemed a very likeable sort of fellow, very much like ourselves, and not at all the sort of man to murder his wife'—that is not reasonable doubt, either."

Against the prisoner, that little homily, surely?

"Finally, a word about circumstantial evidence. There is a widespread impression among the public that circumstantial evidence is not good evidence, but this is by no means necessarily so. Sometimes it is as good and conclusive as the evidence of actual witnesses. But you must apply to circumstantial evidence a rigorous test, and the test is this—does it rule out, in the eyes of any reasonable person, all other theories or possibilities. If it does **not**, then there must be doubt, and if there is doubt the prisoner is entitled to acquittal."

That seemed to redress the balance. The jury were back where they started. Now the fate of Charles Hilary was in their hands.

Kathryn sat hunched in her seat, waiting. She was terrified—so terrified that she could hardly speak. John had wanted her to leave, to spare herself this agony of suspense, but she had seemed not to hear. Of course she had to stay.

Ten minutes passed, twenty minutes, half an hour. Her brother suggested that they should stretch their legs outside as other people were doing, smoke a cigarette, anything to keep themselves from thinking. She shook her head; she couldn't trust herself to move.

Forty minutes, fifty minutes. How long could one be tortured and keep sane? Then, suddenly, there was a distant stirring, a hum of excitement, raised voices, a bustling into seats. God, they were coming back!

"Members of the jury, are you agreed upon your verdict?"

"We are."

"Do you find the prisoner guilty or not guilty?"

"Guilty."

The blood drummed in Kathryn's head. Through a mist she saw Charles draw himself up; heard the judge's voice —"Have you anything to say . . .?" and Charles's cold "Nothing at all". Then ghastly, unbelievable words that would ring forever in her ears, and a sonorous "Amen!" She felt herself falling and clutched her brother's arm and that was the last thing she remembered for quite a while.

Part Two

CHAPTER I

At four o'clock on a Tuesday afternoon—exactly sixteen hours before the time fixed for Charles Hilary's execution—a large petrol lorry was making its way through the south-western suburbs of London. Its driver, a heavily-built man named William Moore, was stripped to the waist in his cabin, for the temperature was ninety-three in the shade and had been over ninety for three days in succession. Moore was suffering badly from the heat—in fact he felt so exhausted that he had decided to go and see the doctor after he had unloaded the cargo of petrol from the huge tank behind him.

As the lorry slowly descended the hill that led to Penton-hurst prison, the big double gates swung open and a car emerged. Moore slowed to let it turn in front of him and was just going to follow it when another car with an L-plate nipped across his off-side wing. With a muttered curse he wrenched the heavy wheel over to avoid a collision—and that was the last thing he ever knew. His grip relaxed, his body slumped in its seat, and his foot wedged down hard on the accelerator. At full throttle, the great lorry gathered speed and roared through the open prison gates. A uniformed officer who was about to shut them gave a shout of alarm, failed to jump aside in time, and was swept under the wheels.

Travelling now at nearly forty miles an hour, the lorry careered across the main courtyard, struck the doorway of one of the prison blocks with a fearful crash, and overturned. The petrol tank, ripped open by the impact, spewed out its contents, and as the fuel reached the hot exhaust there was a violent explosion. In a matter of seconds, Moore's body was incinerated. Two thousand gallons of flaming petrol were flung about the prison and almost before anyone had realised what had happened there was a sea of fire stretching from the point of collision to the hospital block. From a neighbouring store where the material for the mailbags was kept, columns of black smoke began to pour.

When the crash came, Charles was lying on his bed in the roomy cell reserved for the condemned. The thick walls had not sufficed to keep out the phenomenal heat of the day, and he had stripped down to a singlet and underpants and canvas shoes. Even so, he was sweating.

Three weeks had elapsed since the Old Bailey verdict. At first he had permitted himself to hope, for though the lawyers had advised him that the trial had been impeccably conducted and that there was little hope for the appeal, they had thought there was a fair chance of a reprieve. Then, three days ago, had come word that the Home Secretary saw no reason to intervene.

He had been in mental agony for some time after that. To be deprived of the life that had begun to hold such promise, for a crime that he knew nothing about—that was a thought to unhinge the mind. He had lived through a frenzy of rage, a black hell of despair. But with the approach of the last hours he had grown calmer, disciplining himself with trite but eternal truths. Everyone had to die and few were happy in their end. Why rail at injustice when it was the rule of the world, the common experience? Why rail at all, when nothing could be altered? He was going to die, and it was better to die stoically than cravenly. . . .

The worst part had been the farewell to Kathryn. Stoicism grew from contemplation, not from lovers meeting. Face to face, they had gazed at each other in a dumb agony of love and grief. It had been harder, afterwards, to take the cosmic view.

Still, he had forced his mind into acceptance again. When the crash came, he hardly noticed it. He was like a man in a trance, almost impervious to noise and shock.

But the tumult grew more insistent, and presently he roused himself and padded across the floor to the iron grille. Somewhere along the corridor, men were screaming and beating frantically on locked doors. The warder who never ceased to watch him had disappeared. People were pounding past, shouting to each other above the din. Alarm bells were ringing. The orderly routine of the prison had been shattered.

Acrid smoke was seeping along the passage, and Charles began to cough. The pandemonium was increasing, the panic was infectious. Now he could hear the metallic clang of cell doors being flung back. They must be evacuating the block. Instinctively and irrationally he began to beat on his own door.

Then keys jangled, and through a fog of smoke a warder yelled "Out!" and grabbed him by the arm. In a moment he had joined the scurrying throng of prisoners in the corridor. The screaming had got worse—some poor devils must be trapped.

Outside in the courtyard, all was confusion. Two blocks were burning furiously, and a thick blanket of smoke had turned the sun into a dull red ball. Around the hospital building, warders and prisoners were combining in frenzied rescue attempts. Each second their task became more difficult as the smoke settled in the motionless, humid air.

A fire-engine tore through the prison gates and across the yard, nearly running Charles down. He stepped back and stood irresolute while hoses were run out around him. The restraining hand was no longer upon his arm—in this moment of catastrophe, when the uncondemned were being burned alive, he had ceased to be of paramount importance.

The pall of smoke steadily thickened and descended, until soon nothing was visible but vague shadows. People passed close to him, but he didn't know whether they were prisoners or warders, police or firemen. Choking, he moved away to get out of the smoke and as he groped ahead his fingers touched ironwork. Dim shapes were bent over something on the ground—others were milling around the gate, noisy and excited. He walked out and no one stopped him and a moment later he was in the road.

Until now he had had no conscious thought of escape— three months under lock and key had got him out of the habit of acting on his own initiative. But once outside the prison it seemed absurd to go back. He couldn't hope to get far in these clothes, but at least he had nothing to lose. He began to run.

72

As he emerged from the smokescreen into bright sunshine a youth racing by on a bicycle called out derisively, "Keep your elbows in!" For a moment the significance of the words didn't register, but when he received tolerant smiles from other people whom he passed he suddenly realised what was happening. Because of his singlet and underpants they were mistaking him for a real runner—an athlete out for training! He thrust his chest forward and his shoulders back and tried to imitate the easy loping stride of the expert. As long as he kept moving, he could probably maintain the illusion, and if so . . . For the first time, he began to think of escape as a serious possibility, and when an opportunity occurred he turned off the main road. Presently he found himself in a maze of mean streets where children played in the gutters and jeered as he passed.

By now his unpractised legs were beginning to feel weak and his breath was rattling in his dry throat. He couldn't keep this up much longer—if he went on without a pause for rest he would collapse. But if he stopped running, his bizarre appearance would soon bring a crowd round him and at close quarters his prison clothes would give him away. He could think of only one course that offered any hope—to ring up Kathryn. If she could pick him up in her car and take him out of the neighbourhood, there was a chance.

Ahead of him he could see a road junction, with a public lavatory in the middle of it and—yes!—a telephone box. He covered the hundred yards in a final spurt and flung himself into the kiosk. Panting, he grasped the receiver.

It was only then that he realised he had no money. Threepence!—that was all he needed. Three pennies at that moment represented the entrance fee to paradise—and there was nowhere he could get them. In a sudden frenzy he banged at button B, but no magical shower of coppers resulted. He groaned. Surely there was some way!

Then he remembered that it was sometimes possible to transfer the charge for a call, and hope returned. For a second or two he stood with his hand on the receiver, getting his breath back, thinking what he would say to the operator, what he would say to Kathryn if he got through. Then he dialled o. By the time the operator answered, his voice was under control.

"I want to make a transferred charge call to Flaxman 48042. I haven't any change."

The girl took it quite as a matter of course. "What is your name, please?"

"Forrester. John Forrester."

"Hold the line."

Almost at once the phone began to ring at the other end. It rang and rang—but nothing happened.

She's not there, he thought in bitter despair, and sweat poured into his eyes. He had been afraid of this. She had been ill after the trial and when she had visited him in prison she had looked utterly exhausted. She had probably gone away somewhere—she might even be *with* John at this moment . . . .

Suddenly there was a click and the ringing stopped. He heard the operator talking and then, like music from heaven, Kathryn's voice.

"Go ahead, caller," said the girl cheerfully.

He didn't think anyone would be listening in but it seemed wiser to take no risks. He plunged at once into his prepared piece.

"Kathryn!—before you say a single word let me tell you how frightfully sorry I am that I wasn't able to keep that appointment today. Something quite extraordinary happened and it completely changed my plans. You do understand, don't you? But I'm free now, quite free, and I'm at a place called Porter Street, S.W.17, where it joins Lemon Street. Do you think you could possibly pick me up here right away?"

"There was a moment's absolute silence—then a frightened sibilance rather than a word.

"Charles!"

He tried to sound matter-of-fact. "Porter Street and Lemon Street. Could you come?"

Again a pause, and then—"Yes, oh yes."

"Right. I'll expect you in about half an hour. In case I'm getting a cup of tea or something, will you give a hoot when you reach the junction?"

"Yes." Her voice, though still low, had more assurance. "I'll come at once."

He hung up quickly and looked out through the glass doors. Two men and a woman were passing on the other

74

side of the street. He watched them out of sight and let a car go by and then he made a dash for the flight of steps marked "Gentlemen." The lavatory, like the district, was grimy, and there was no attendant. One of the closets had the word "Free" on it and he slipped inside and shut the door.

At last, a respite!

While he waited, he considered the next move. His immediate needs were clear enough. Clothes, food—above all, somewhere safe to hide. Somewhere off the beaten track, where he could lie undisturbed until the first fury of the manhunt was over. Somewhere where there was no possibility of his being seen by a soul, for by tomorrow his face would be as well known as Kathryn's and everyone would be against him. He thought he knew the very place, if only he could get there. It would mean involving Kathryn deeply, but any move would do that. . . . A plan of action began to take shape in his mind.

After a while he heard a church clock strike in the distance. Five o'clock—he must have been down here at least half an hour. He tried hard to curb his impatience, telling himself that Kathryn had the rush-hour traffic to contend with and that finding a rendezvous like this wouldn't be easy for her and that it was amazing she had the strength to come at all. But it was difficult to keep calm—this place wasn't really safe. Every few minutes someone came down the steps and once there was a tentative push at the door behind which he crouched. At every fresh alarm, his heart seemed to turn over. With freedom, even this much freedom, fear had come back. Once again, he had something to lose.

Suddenly, almost overhead, a familiar hooter summoned him. Thank God!—she'd done it! He opened the door a fraction of an inch and stood listening. Everything seemed quiet. He emerged cautiously and mounted the steps, ready to retreat on the instant if anyone should appear. Through the railings he could see the buff car, and Kathryn pale and alert behind the wheel. A lorry turned into the junction and he ducked and waited until it had gone by. Then he dived across the road.

At the sound of his step Kathryn twisted round in her seat. She hardly knew what she had been expecting—the shock of hearing his voice on the telephone had almost paralysed thought and his message had been utterly bewildering. It had been enough that in some miraculous way he seemed to have been set free. Now, as she caught sight of his clothes, consternation showed in her face.

He jerked the door open and flung himself into the rear seat. "Drive on, Kathryn!—quickly! Make for the Elephant . . .!"

As the car moved off her eyes met his in the driving mirror and it was like the meeting of ghosts. "My darling!" she said in a choking voice. "Oh, my darling!" Her mind was in a desperate tangle—there seemed no words for a situation like this. "Charles—what's happened?"

"The prison caught fire. I escaped."

Escaped! Suddenly everything fell into place. She felt no astonishment at that moment—only a fierce excitement, an eager acceptance of the challenge. Her face became a mask of concentration as she mentally worked out her route. Behind her, Charles tried to compress himself into a smaller space, fearful that someone might notice his strange garb and afterwards remember the car.

"Listen, Kathryn," he said tensely, "before you get any deeper into this you've got to realise something—you could get ten years for helping me. I shouldn't have brought you into it at all—I didn't want to, but I couldn't think of any other way. . . ."

"Traffic lights!" she said sharply. "Keep down. There should be a rug there."

He found it and covered himself as the car stopped.

Directly they were over the crossing Kathryn said: "My darling, the only thing we have to think about now is how to keep you alive. We're in this together and you can count on me absolutely—you know that. I simply don't care what happens to me. Now—where do you want me to take you? What about my flat?—couldn't you hide there?"

"No, that'll be the first place they'll search. The moment they miss me they'll be after you—they'll know I can't manage without you, not in these clothes and without any money. Besides, I've got to keep right away from people. I think the Medway's the best place."

76

"The cottage?"

"Not for me—they'll remember that that was our hide-out. I thought of Twinney Island. I could camp out there indefinitely."

She gave a murmur of assent. Twinney Island was one of a complex group of islets and tide-swept saltings in the big southern bulge of the Medway where they had spent so many week-ends. It had a battered sea-wall round it that would give some protection and it was only a quarter of a mile or so from the cottage. It was as wild and desolate a spot as any in the country.

She accelerated past a bus, watching her speedometer. Responsibility lay heavy upon her—she must hurry, but it would be fatal to be stopped for speeding. "What about supplies?" she asked.

"We must get everything over tonight, before the police come. There's plenty of stuff at the cottage."

That was true. There were lots of tins of food that they'd collected for the holiday in *Witch* and hadn't used, and many other things that Charles would need as well.

"Can I come to the island with you?"

"That's not possible, darling—the police would find the car. Besides, you'll be my only lifeline. Sooner or later, everything may depend on your keeping your freedom of movement."

"What shall I do, then?"

"Well, it's a bit tricky, but I think the safest thing would be for you to stay on at the cottage for a day or two. The point is, the police are bound to ask where you were from five o'clock this afternoon onwards and I don't see how you can possibly invent a watertight story to cover six or seven hours. They can't prove anything if they find you staying quite openly at the cottage, but if you say you haven't been there and then they discover you have they'll know for certain the visit was something to do with me."

"Yes, I see that. I can always say I've come down to get away from people—that sounds reasonable enough. The only thing is, if they find me there they might get suspicious and think of the islands."

"If they do, that'll be the end of me, but somehow I don't think they will. What they will do is to watch you, because they'll argue that if I'm around I'll be dependent upon you for supplies and keeping an eye on you will be the easiest way of checking up. When they discover that you're just staying put and behaving quite naturally, they'll probably decide I'm not there. At least, that's how I see it."

"I hope you're right. Better get down again, darling—we're just coming to the Elephant and the lights are red."

The traffic was at its height at the busy junction and they were held up for nearly five minutes. It was stifling under the rug, but the pavements were crowded and Charles didn't dare to raise his head. When at last they moved off along the New Kent Road, Kathryn gave a quick look round.

"All right, darling?"

"Just about."

"What's the plan, then? Shall I row you out first and then bring the stuff from the cottage afterwards?"

"No, I think I'd better keep away from the place altogether. I don't suppose for a moment there'll be anyone about, but it'll still be broad daylight when we get there and there's no point in taking unnecessary risks. What I suggest is that you drop me just beyond East Rainham where the road touches the sea-wall—by Otterham Creek, you remember?—and I'll lie low there until dusk. Then I'll walk round the sea wall and swim to the island."

She thought of the swift tides and the muddy banks and the total lack of seamarks in that part of the estuary. Still, Charles was a good swimmer and there were so many ways in which disaster might overtake them that there really wasn't much sense in worrying about minor dangers.

"All right," she said, "but for heaven's sake be careful. Now tell me exactly what I must do."

"Well, after you've dropped me you'll drive on to the cottage and load up the dinghy and as soon as the tide is right you'll row out to the island and put the stuff ashore. Then you'll take the dinghy back and prepare to put on a good act when the visitors arrive."

"Suppose the tide's out all night?"

"We must hope it won't be," said Charles. One thing was certain—it would be quite impossible to manhandle the stores across the mud if the creek were dry.

"I'd feel happier if we knew. I believe there's a *Times* on the ledge by the rear window—not terribly old."

78

Charles raised his head cautiously. After a little fumbling he found the paper and turned up the meteorological report, as he'd done so often in the past when they'd been setting off on one of their trips. He noted the time of high water at London Bridge and made a rough calculation.

"Our luck's in," he said. "High water at the cottage should be around ten-thirty."

Kathryn relaxed with a sigh. "That means I'll be able to leave about half past nine."

"Yes, but you'll have to make quite sure there's enough water to float the dinghy comfortably, or it'll leave marks in the mud. The police are certain to look, and if they discover you've used the boat they're bound to think of the islands. I'm afraid it may mean ferrying the things across in the dark. . . ." He remembered with a pang of self-reproach that she was still a convalescent. "It's going to be tough, darling. Do you feel up to it?"

"I feel fine," she said confidently. "It's been better than a blood transfusion, being together again. . . . Anyway, it'll be much safer after dark."

"That's true. And we shall probably reach the island at about the same time."

"I do hope so. I'd hate not to see you settled in. Oh, darling, I *wish* I could stay there with you."

"For once in my life, sweetheart, I don't. It's going to be bad enough living like a hunted savage myself, without dragging you into it."

For a few moments the task of coping with the traffic and picking out the route through south London preoccupied her. Then she said, "Couldn't we fix up some sort of signalling system so that we can keep in touch?"

"I don't see how. I shan't dare to show my head above the island wall in daylight, and I certainly couldn't use a light at night."

"But I could—we could have some arrangement about the cottage lights so that I could warn you if there was any special danger, or let you know when the coast was clear. After all, we've got to arrange to meet again some time."

"Yes, but I don't like the idea of signalling with lights—the police will be watching for just that sort of thing, and they're pretty smart. I'll keep a good look-out and I shall

79

see when they leave. I'd sooner improvise when the time comes."

"All right, if you're sure." Kathryn negotiated the junction at New Cross Gate and turned eastwards. In half an hour, now, they would be out of London. As soon as the traffic thinned a little she said: "Tell me what to put in the dinghy, besides food."

"Water's the chief thing—better fill a couple of those old jerrycans out of the shed. Clothes, of course—there's an old pair of shorts and some bush shirts—just the right protective colouring. My jacket and sweater, if there's room in the dinghy—you'll have to see. I'd better have the wellingtons, in case I have to do any walking about in the mud. The Zeiss glasses, too, if I'm to keep an eye on the place. Oh, and a tin-opener—don't forget that, whatever you do. I wouldn't like to starve in the midst of plenty!"

Kathryn's eyes flicked anxiously to the mirror. "Darling, what will happen when your food is all gone? How can I bring you more if they're watching me all the time?"

"You can't—we've got to face that. If you make one move in my direction or even so much as squint at the islands they'll be on to me like a shot. But if you cram the dinghy full I ought to be able to manage for a week or ten days—perhaps longer at a pinch—and by that time the hunt may have shifted."

"I'll be dead with worry if it hasn't. Anyhow, I'll put in everything there is." She drove silently for a while, mentally reviewing the stores at the cottage. Presently she said: "How long do you think it will be before the police come?"

"A few hours, at least. The prison was a shambles—they can't possibly take a roll-call yet." He had begun to sound very tired—he was feeling the reaction now after all the effort and excitement. "God, that was a frightful thing, Kathryn—I'm only just beginning to realise how frightful it was. I don't know what caused it, but whatever it was it all happened in a matter of seconds. There were people being burned to death, but at the time it made no impression on me. It was just as though I were sleep-walking until I found myself outside the prison—actually outside, and in the street. I suppose I could have done something to help if I'd stayed—or could I? Probably they'd have shut me up again pretty soon. . . ."

"Don't worry about that, darling. If ever anyone was entitled to take his chance, you were."

He sighed and lay back against the seat. He still had to keep the rug handy, but there were fewer stops for lights now and the traffic was much less troublesome. Soon they would be out in the country. Kathryn had put on speed and was giving all her attention to her driving. It was some time before she spoke again.

"Charles, I'll have to stop somewhere and fill up with petrol—we've only about half a gallon left."

"All right," he said calmly. "Better make it soon—we mustn't run out."

"We're coming to a garage now."

"I'll keep down, then." Once more he squeezed into the well between the seats and drew the rug over him.

Kathryn gave a quick glance round to make sure he was completely covered and then pulled in beside the pumps. It was only after she had stopped the car that she saw there was an A.A. scout there as well as the garage man.

"Four gallons, please," she called through the open window.

The garage man nodded and carried the pipe round to the tank. The A.A. scout stood looking at the front of the car for a moment and then sidled up to the window with a friendly grin.

"Evening, miss. Do I gather you're not a member of the A.A.?"

She flung a concealing arm along the back of the seat, wishing she had chosen any garage but this. If he were to see the rug move . . . !

"I belong to the R.A.C."

"Yes, so I see, and a very good organisation it is. All the same, how often do you meet an R.A.C. patrol on the road, compared with an A.A.? Now if you belonged to both . . ." He produced some literature and embarked on a line of persuasive sales talk. Kathryn smiled up at him, anxious to keep his whole attention focused on her.

The pump stopped whirring and she gave the garage man a pound note, praying that he'd hurry. She would have liked to tell him to keep the change, but it was too much for a tip and he might think it odd.

"Well, I'm afraid I can't decide about it now," she told the A.A. man. She started the engine. "I'm in rather a hurry."

"That's all right, miss—just think it over." The scout stepped back, looked at her for a moment with a curious expression, and then came to the window again. "Excuse me, but you wouldn't be Miss Kathryn Forrester, would you?"

She took her change. "I would, yes . . ."

"I thought I recognised you . . ." Then his face grew solemn, and she knew that he wasn't thinking of television any more, but of the trial. It was the usual thing, these days—the smile of pleasure, and then the afterthought. She gave a brief nod and drove quickly out into the road.

Charles struggled out from under the rug, crimson-faced. "God, I was afraid we'd never get away!" he said.

"Wasn't it awful? Thank goodness you kept still."

The open road lay ahead of them now, and the rest of the journey passed quickly and without incident. It was just before seven when they ran into Rochester. With a growing sense of excitement, Kathryn swung the car over the bridge that spanned the Medway and turned eastwards through Chatham and Gillingham along familiar streets. Not long now. Her thoughts had become entirely practical. The sooner she could get those stores to the island, the sooner Charles would be safe.

Presently they branched off along a minor road that skirted the southern shore of the estuary. As the houses became more scattered, Charles's own spirits began to rise. They were moving into quiet, empty country, and every inch of it was well known to him. If there had to be a hunt, he couldn't have wished for more friendly terrain. It looked as though they were going to be lucky with the weather, too, for the sun was sinking in a clear sky with the promise of another fine day tomorrow."

They slipped through the tiny village of East Rainham and approached the spot where the road and the sea-wall converged. Charles looked carefully around to make sure there were no other cars in sight.

"All right," he said, "this is it. We'd better make it snappy while the road's clear."

She stopped the car and turned. "Good-bye, my love. Kiss me."

He leaned over and touched her lips with his own. "Don't worry, darling—it may not be for long. I'll find some way of seeing you."

"And I'll get those things to you somehow."

"Bless you!" He got swiftly out of the car and without a backward glance climbed the low sea-wall and disappeared from sight. Kathryn pulled the door shut after him and drove on towards the cottage.

CHAPTER II

CREEK COTTAGE—"Hilary's love-nest", as one of the Sunday newspapers had called it after the trial—was a rather ugly two-storey brick house with a small sitting-room and scullery downstairs and two tiny bedrooms upstairs. It conspicuously lacked all modern conveniences. Water had to be fetched from a brackish well two hundred yards away; cooking, if any, was by paraffin stove; lighting was by oil lamps. Raised above the surrounding saltings on a narrow peninsula of higher ground, it could be reached from the road only along a rough causeway which itself was submerged at the top of high spring tides. In winter it was battered by fierce salt winds; in summer it was scorched by shadeless heat. For twenty years, until Charles had bought it, it had stood empty and derelict, and not even the locals could remember why it had been built.

It was Peter Challock, Charles's ex-colleague at the Colonial Office, who during a week-end sail in *Witch* had first been struck by the possibilities of the place as a retreat. He had taken Charles and Kathryn to look at it and they had both agreed that it could be the solution of their immediate problem. A local solicitor had managed to discover the name of the owner and, without difficulty, persuaded him to sell. A builder from Rochester had patched up the roof and window frames and floors, and redecorated it. In a few weeks the house had been made fit to live in once more. Kathryn had bought some second-hand furniture and had taken pleasure in making the place as comfortable as possible.

It had been, of course, a week-end base rather than a home; a place to visit and make sorties from rather than to linger in. Nevertheless, for a time Charles and Kathryn had found it the perfect sanctuary and an ideal holiday spot in good weather. They had bought a sixteen-foot cabin

84

boat called *Spray* from a friend of Peter's and during fine spells had picnicked and explored all over the estuary. They had never pretended to be anything but fair-weather sailors, but some skill had come with experience and in the end they had taken pride in their ability to negotiate the tortuous creeks and saltings without mishap. On rare occasions they had even ventured out to sea. In cold or rainy weather they had made themselves as cosy as they could indoors, burning driftwood in the little iron grate. The cottage was so remote that they had felt completely cut off from the world. Sometimes a shallow-draught boat would work its way down through the islands on a summer's day, but it could never stay long because the creek had water in it only for an hour or two around high water. From the landward side, no one ever approached.

Week-end after week-end Kathryn had lived like a gipsy down here before hurrying back to London to take a luxurious bath and repair the damage to her hands and become again a well-groomed television star. It had been rough and tough, and in the weeks that had preceded Charles's arrest she had had to admit to herself that the cottage and the creek and the camping-out life were beginning to lose a good deal of their magic for her. There had come a day, indeed, when she had said to Charles, in a moment of extreme fatigue, "I don't think I can go on being a girl guide for ever, you know...."

But all that lay in the past—the past that in retrospect seemed happy and carefree. Now, as Kathryn brought the car to a halt beside the peeling front door and sat for a moment looking out over the desolate scene, her thoughts were solely of the task ahead. She had been a little worried in case something might have happened to the dinghy during their long absence, but a glance set her fears at rest. It was still there in the mud, secured by a long painter to a post driven into a patch of shingle. *Spray* was there, too, sitting almost upright on her duck-belly and looking little the worse for three months of neglect. There was no water in the creek yet—only an expanse of glistening brown ooze and green weed that stretched away past the chain of islands to the distant deep channel.

She collected the door key from under the stone where they had left it all those weeks ago and let herself in. The place smelt as musty as a vault and she flung the windows wide open. From a cupboard in one of the bedrooms she took the tarpaulin-wrapped bundle in which the sleeping-bags and pillows and boating clothes were kept, and changed into slacks and a sweater. Then she fetched her rubber boots from the lean-to wooden shed, and set to work.

Getting water was always a laborious job, for the rusty iron pump worked only spasmodically. She took the car, and filled the two jerrycans and a lidded enamel pail for herself. The cans still smelt of petrol even after she had rinsed them several times, but she had no other containers. Back at the cottage she put them outside the door on the baked earth and began to pile the other things beside them. The things that Charles had particularly asked for, first, so that she wouldn't overlook them—his old clothes, his sea-boots, his binoculars, and—in case the weather turned bad—his sleeping-bag and the tarpaulin.

Then she began to carry out the tins of food from the pantry. There was meat of sorts and fish in dull variety; a little tinned butter and cheese and bacon, and an assortment of soups. There were three tins of Trinidad guavas, which Charles had bought specially because she liked them, but there was no other fruit—they had still been in the middle of their preparations when the arrest had ended everything. He would have plenty of condensed milk, but no fresh milk; a few packets of biscuits, but no bread; no vegetables or green salad; no eggs. It was going to be a pretty thin diet, she reflected, for a healthy man living an open-air life. However, there was nothing she could do about it. She kept back a little tea and sugar and a tin of condensed milk but she brought out everything else that there was, and last of all the tin opener.

Every time she emerged she cast an apprehensive glance around the horizon. If the police were to descend on her now, while all these things were spread out on the ground, they would know at once what she was up to. But the emptiness of the scene was reassuring, and so was the wide view. In this flat, treeless place there was at least no danger of being taken by surprise. She could see for a mile in every direction, and nothing moved but birds.

When she had stacked the tins she went carefully

86

through the house and shed, gathering up anything that might prove useful to a hunted Crusoe. She picked out an enamel plate and mug that wouldn't be missed; a knife and fork and spoon; a jack-knife; a little chopper that Charles had used for splitting firewood; a pair of scissors, and a bottle of detergent that would make a good lather in salt water. Matches were a problem—there were none in the cottage, and the only ones she had in her bag were a few book matches. She tore off a couple for herself and put the rest in an old envelope together with the eight cigarettes from her case. She wondered if she should give him the paraffin stove but decided that the police might think it strange if the cottage had no means of heating anything. Finally she added a chart of the Medway, two or three paper-backed novels, and an old rug from the sitting-room.

Dusk was beginning to fall by the time she had finished. The tide had started to creep in over the mud but it still hadn't reached the dinghy and for the moment there was nothing more she could do. She sat down on the ground outside the cottage and regarded the pile of stores. She didn't think she had forgotten anything important, but it would be awful if she had. She wondered how Charles was getting on behind his sea-wall, and when he had last eaten. If only, she wished again, she could have shared the rigours of the next few days with him. She gazed across at the low dark outline of Twinney Island, and it looked lonely and comfortless. The dying day threw a melancholy light over the creek, and she shivered. Waiting was the worst part.

Presently she gave a tentative pull on the dinghy painter and felt the boat stir. In a few moments it was floating clear of the mud and she drew it in until its forefoot grounded gently on the shingle. It was half full of water, which was something she hadn't reckoned on. As she baled it out with an old tin she realised that she must put some water back into it afterwards, or the police would know she'd used it. There was so much to remember—and it would be so easy to make a mistake.

After she had mopped out the bilges with a rag she was ready to load the stores. There was hard earth or shingle all the way from the cottage to the boat so there was no risk of leaving tell-tale marks. She had to stow everything very carefully, for the dinghy was only seven feet long and she must leave room for herself.

She gave a sigh of thankfulness when it was done. In an hour from now, with any luck, she'd have delivered her cargo and seen Charles safely installed. The dinghy would be tied up again and she'd be ready to face all comers. Impatiently she waited for the last of the daylight to fade. Charles must be on the point of setting off on his walk now and it would take him half an hour. She ought to be making a move herself. She went to the shed and fetched the oars and rowlocks.

She was just about to push off from the shingle when she saw a light flashing on the main road a mile or more away. It grew brighter and suddenly, to her horror, resolved itself into the twin beams of headlamps pointing straight towards her. A car was coming along the causeway!

For a moment she stood petrified, holding the oar. It could only be the police—no one else would come to this spot, and at night. Her heart thumped as she struggled to fight down her panic. *What should she do?* She couldn't go off with the dinghy now—they'd see her car there and guess what she was doing and wait for her, and if she didn't come back they'd search the neighbourhood. But it would be just as bad if they found the dinghy like this. With a sick feeling she dropped the oars across the thwarts, stepped out on to the shingle, and pushed the boat away from the shore with all her strength. The tide caught it, it swung round once or twice, and then slowly drifted away into the darkness.

Already the car was half-way along the raised track and she knew she hadn't a moment to lose. Frantically she dashed to the shed, flung her rubber boots into a corner, and shut the door. Then, barefooted, she ran to the cottage, groped her way upstairs in the darkness, and hurriedly changed back into her town frock and smart shoes. She rolled up the slacks and sweater and tossed them into the cupboard, raced downstairs again and lit the sitting-room lamp, ran a comb through her hair, and tried to compose herself.

She heard the car pulled up and the voices of two men talking in low, conspiratorial tones. They seemed to be

88

reconnoitring outside. There was the unmistakable sound of the shed door being opened and of a car door being slammed—her own, she thought. Feet crunched menacingly on the shingle. She suddenly realised that the part of innocence required her to resent this noisy and unexplained intrusion and she went quickly to the door. As she opened it, one of the men flashed a torch straight into her eyes, and she gave an involuntary cry.

"Miss Forrester?"

"Who are you?" she demanded indignantly. "What on earth do you think you're doing, prowling about there?"

The torch probed the empty corners of the sitting-room and the men seemed to relax a little. "Sorry to trouble you, miss—we're from the county police. Fellows is my name—Detective-Sergeant Fellowes." The sergeant had a youthful, pleasant voice, and as he lowered the torch she could see that he had a pleasant face as well. "Are you alone?"

"Yes, I am. Why?"

"Do you mind if we take a look round the house?"

"What for? What's the matter?"

Fellowes hesitated. "Haven't you heard the news, miss?"

"I haven't heard anything."

"Why, Charles Hilary escaped from prison this afternoon."

"Escaped!" Kathryn saw the chance of a breathing space. For a moment she gazed at him incredulously, clutching the doorpost for support. Then, slowly and very competently, she crumpled to the floor.

When she opened her eyes after a suitable interval, the sergeant was bending over her solicitously, a glass of water in his hand. She had heard the other man go upstairs—his heavy footfalls were still audible in the room above and she caught the sound of a cupboard being opened. For a moment she feared he might notice that the slacks and sweater were damp, but he was down again almost at once, flashing his torch round the scullery.

"All clear, Sarge—nothing here."

Fellowes dabbed water on Kathryn's forehead with his fingertips and put the glass down. "That was a nasty tumble, miss. Feeling better, now?"

"Yes—thank you."

"Bit of a shock for you, I'm afraid."

Kathryn nodded, and struggled to sit up. "What happened—about Charles, I mean? How did he manage to get away?"

The policeman took a paper from his pocket and gave it to her. It was a late edition of the *News*, its front page black with headlines. "Fire at Pentonhurst," she read. "Heavy Casualties in Prison Blaze." "Charles Hilary Escapes."

"Oh, God!" she murmured. She looked up at Fellowes. "Did you think he was here?"

"Well, miss, we had to make sure." The sergeant sounded quite apologetic. "I expect you'd like to be left alone now. I'll have to station the constable outside, but he won't disturb you." He turned at the door. "It might be better if you stayed up for a while, though, Miss Forrester—an inspector will probably be coming down from the Yard to see you." He nodded, and went out. A moment later she heard the car drive away.

The thought of the lost dinghy still lay like a black shadow on her mind but there was no time to waste in the contemplation of disaster. The sergeant had merely been the outrider—if an inspector were coming down it meant she was going to be questioned closely, and there were still things to be done. She turned the lamp up a little and went outside to get her can of water. The constable, who was standing on the shingle looking out over the creek, directed his torch on her suspiciously, but switched it off when he saw what she was doing. She went in and shut the door.

Behind drawn curtains, she washed her hands and face and applied new make-up. Her nails were grubby, and she cleaned them carefully and polished them. So were the soles of her feet, and she washed those too. Then she went upstairs to the cupboard and carefully examined the slacks and sweater. They *were* slightly damp, but the state of the house could account for that and at least there was no wet mud on them. When she had satisfied herself that she had done everything possible by way of precaution, she made herself a cup of tea and settled down to think out what she would say.

. . . . .

It was nearly midnight when sounds from the causeway told her that the police were coming back. This time there seemed to be two cars. She heard Fellowes's voice as he spoke to the constable, and another one that was vaguely familiar, and she waited tensely for the knock. When it came, the man standing in the doorway was Inspector Bates.

"Come in," she said.

"Thank you." The inspector dropped his hat on the settee and gave her a long, searching look. "Well, Miss Forrester, this is a very unfortunate business—very tragic and distressing for you, very disturbing for us. I wish we could have spared you this extra strain. . . . Still, there it is, we have our duty to do." His manner became brisker. "Now tell me, do you know where Hilary is?"

"If I did," she said, "you may be quite sure I shouldn't tell you—but as a matter of fact I don't."

"Has he been in communication with you?"

"No."

"You realise, Miss Forrester, that the penalties for helping a convicted murderer can be very severe?"

"Nothing worse could happen to me than has happened already," she said. "But as I say, I don't know anything. The first I heard of it was when Sergeant Fellowes called."

"We shall have to satisfy ourselves about that. Hilary escaped in his vest and underpants. It's almost incredible that he wasn't picked up right away, but he wasn't, and now he seems to have gone to ground. He couldn't have done that without help. Can you think of anyone in the world who would assist him—except yourself?"

"He had many friends."

"I should be very surprised to learn that any of them would risk imprisonment to help him at this stage. In your case, of course, it's different. When did you come down here?"

"I left home at about five this afternoon and got down at about seven."

"What made you come?"

"Charles and I had lived here together. I felt I should like to be here when he—when he died."

Bates looked, and was, uncomfortable. It would have been much better, he thought, if she had gone to stay with relatives or friends for the night, but that was hardly his business. "I'm sorry I have to intrude like this," he said, "but I'm afraid it's quite unavoidable. Was it your intention to stay long?"

"I hadn't any intention. I just came—I suddenly couldn't bear it in London any longer. If you mean did I bring anything with me, I didn't, not a thing. I simply wanted to get here. I should probably have gone back tomorrow."

"Will you still go back tomorrow?"

"I don't know." She looked at him, and suddenly her expression changed. "I suppose that's what you want me to do," she said bitterly. "You'd like me to go there because you know that's where he'll probably make for. You want me to be the decoy. Well, I won't. If you catch him, it's not going to be through me."

Bates grunted. "What have you been doing since you got here?"

Her defiance seemed to wilt, and she looked as though she were going to cry. "What would you have been doing if someone you loved was going to be hanged in the morning? I wasn't doing anything—I was just sitting. God knows I've plenty to think about."

The inspector struggled against his natural feelings—in his long career he couldn't remember a job he had found more distasteful. "May I see your hands?" he said.

"My hands?" She held them out and he examined them under the lamp.

"Now your shoes."

She slipped them off and he scrutinised them carefully before handing them back. Then he walked to the window and looked out over the dark estuary.

"You and Hilary did some sailing here, didn't you?"

"Yes."

"What boat did you use?"

"A little cabin sailing boat. It's out there now in the mud."

"Is that the only boat you have?"

"Yes."

"I was under the impression that people who sailed always had a—what do you call it?—a dinghy?"

"*Spray* doesn't need one—she only draws a foot and a half, so we managed."

92

"I don't quite follow you," said Bates, who was no yachtsman.

"Well, the whole idea of a dinghy is to get ashore from a bigger boat that has to stay out in deep water, but *Spray* draws so little that we could always walk ashore."

"I see . . . Well, I'd better have a look round."

Once again she listened to footsteps overhead, to the opening of cupboard doors, and, after he had gone out, to the sound of the shed door being opened and shut. There was more conversation outside, and then Bates returned to the sitting-room.

"I see you've a pair of rubber boots in the shed," he said.

"Yes."

"How is it they're wet?"

"I wore them when I went to fetch water from the pump."

"It must be rather muddy round there."

"It is."

"Didn't Hilary have any boots?"

"Yes, but he lost them the last time we went out in *Spray*. He put them out on the mud so that they wouldn't dirty the boat, and forgot about them. The tide came in and carried them away."

"You're very ready with your answers, Miss Forrester."

"It's easy to be when you're telling the truth."

"I found some old clothes of yours upstairs, but none of Hilary's."

"I don't know anything about that. Perhaps he took them away with him. It's a long time since they were used."

"There is only one sleeping-bag."

"He preferred a rug or blankets. He thought sleeping-bags were stuffy."

"I don't see any rug or blankets."

"We used to bring them down with us each time. They only got damp if they were left here."

"Didn't your sleeping bag get damp?"

"No, it's waterproof."

Bates regarded her thoughtfully for a moment, then picked up his hat. "Very well, Miss Forrester, that's all for the time being. I apologise again for having inflicted all this on you. Good night."

93

"Good night, Inspector."

There were more sounds of activity after he had left her. One of the policemen seemed to be going out to *Spray*—from the window she could see his torch waving about in the air as he floundered through the mud, and presently its probing beam lit up the hull and cabin. He was soon back, though, and there was a short conference at the edge of the shingle. They were studying the mud—one of them was bending down. It was just as well, she thought, that she had been careful about floating the dinghy in.

At last the conference broke up and she heard an engine being started. For one wildly hopeful moment she thought that Bates had accepted her story and that they were all going to leave. But only one of the cars drove away. She could see the glow of the constable's cigarette behind the wheel of the other as he settled to his vigil. It was just as Charles had said—they would never leave her!

With a feeling of utter despair, she threw herself on the settee. She wouldn't be able to get any fresh supplies out to him. He was there on the island now, without clothes, without food, without even water—helpless! Thirst would drive him ashore tomorrow. Even if it didn't, someone would be sure to find the loaded dinghy floating in the river and it would be reported and the police would know all they wanted to know. Everything had been in vain. Her overwrought nerves suddenly gave way, and she sobbed as though her heart would break.

CHAPTER III

SOON after nine o'clock Charles had left his grassy hide-out under the sea-wall and started his solitary walk round the edge of the creek. Because it was still not quite dark he avoided the exposed top of the wall, preferring to pick his way through the debris along the shore rather than risk a silhouette against the western sky. Each step required extreme care, for the soles of his canvas shoes were thin and the crackling beach bristled with old tins and spiky lumps of wood and broken glass. He had to be on his guard, too, against putting a foot beyond the dry fringe and leaving prints in the moist ground below the last high-water mark.

There was only one physical obstacle to be negotiated, and that right at the beginning of his journey—the wharf of a small cement works that lay across his path. He approached it with caution in case there should be a night watchman on duty but the place seemed deserted and he got by without incident. There were no more hazards, and as the shore line swung away from the road he ceased to worry about the possibility that someone might see him above the wall. Progress became smoother, and after twenty minutes of steady plodding he drew abreast of Twinney Island. His timing, he saw, was about right—the creek was almost full.

He was now no more than half a mile from the cottage, but darkness had fallen, and all he could make out was a faint glow from one of the windows. The light puzzled him a little—Kathryn would have been wiser, he felt, to wait until she had transported the stores before lighting the lamp. Still, she must know what she was doing. He thought no more about it and concentrated on his own task. Using tufts of coarse grass as stepping stones he made his way out to the end of a half-inundated peninsula, and after a last look round to fix his bearings he quietly committed himself to the creek.

Any uneasiness he might have felt about the crossing itself was soon dispelled. The water was milk-warm, the tide was slack, and he had no heavy clothes to impede his movements. Using the breast stroke to conserve his strength he quickly reduced the gap, and in a moment or two the dark outline of the island wall rose above him. He swam parallel to the bank, reconnoitring the shallows for a suitable landing place. Presently, testing the bottom with his hands, he found a patch of hard gravel and scrambled ashore. He climbed to the top of the wall and dropped to the grass to recover his breath.

The lamp was still burning in the cottage but there were no other signs of life. With a slight sense of disquiet, he listened for the sound of oars. It was strange, he thought, that Kathryn hadn't already arrived—she should have had plenty of time to make her preparations and if she didn't come soon the tide would turn and she would have to row her heavy load against the ebb. Still, she would probably be leaving at any moment now. He decided that when she came he would direct her round to the "hard" he had discovered, where they would be able to unload the stores without leaving marks.

When the minutes continued to slip by without sight or sound of the boat or any movement from the shore, he became deeply worried. This wasn't like Kathryn—something serious must have happened to upset the time-table. His mind was suddenly filled with dire imaginings. Perhaps she had overloaded the dinghy and had an accident! Perhaps the physical strain of the job had been too much for her, and she'd collapsed. She might be lying in the sitting-room now, needing his help. The mere possibility sent him scrambling down from the wall. At least it wouldn't take him long to swim across and find out.

At that moment the lights of a stationary car blazed out beside the cottage. He checked himself at the water's edge, relieved but baffled. It looked, after all, as though no harm had come to her—but what on earth could she be up to? Then he saw two figures move across the light beam—the figures of two men—and the dreadful truth burst upon him.

96

Kathryn had been forestalled by the police. The dinghy wouldn't come. The whole plan had failed.

For a while, he too gave way to despair. The disaster seemed complete and irretrievable. The police must have discovered her preparations and guessed her intentions. At first light they would search for him—and when they found him, Kathryn would be hopelessly compromised. He had done the one thing he was most anxious to avoid—he had sacrificed her in the attempt to save himself.

The thought was unendurable and it spurred him to new action. He had got her into this mess—now he had got to get her out of it. He could think of only one way. If he were captured at some place far from the Medway, and swore that he had never seen her, the police wouldn't be able to prove her complicity. She would certainly not have admitted anything yet, for his sake, and there was no reason why she should ever have to. She could always say that she had loaded up the dinghy in the expectation that he would ultimately make his way to the cottage, and they would hardly charge her with an intention. . . . Yes, that was the way—to put as many miles as possible between himself and her before daybreak.

The thing was, how could he hope to get out of the district in his present state?

Desperate expedients began to suggest themselves. He thought of swimming on from island to island until he reached one of the larger creeks where, at this time of year, commissioned yachts were sometimes left untended at their moorings. If he could get hold of a boat he might well be out of the river by morning. But the chances were that he would tire before he found anything—and even if he were lucky, the fact that the boat had been taken from the Medway would be enough to implicate Kathryn. No, that wouldn't do.

The only other possibility was to return to the mainland and keep moving. It would be a hard slog to get out of the neighbourhood—he wouldn't dare to steal a car or a bicycle, even if at this late hour he had the opportunity, because he didn't want to do anything that might afterwards suggest he had been here. But he had a notion that if he could get as far as Rochester he might be able to smuggle himself into the back of some lorry in the dark, and leave the district that way, and give the driver the slip before he was spotted. If only he had some clothes! Everyone must have heard about the prison break by now, and if he were once seen in his vest and pants, that would be the end. Almost anything would do—clothes off a scarecrow, clothes off a clothes-line. . . .

He stood hesitating under the wall, watching the car drive off along the causeway. Why was it leaving, if it was a police car? It seemed scarcely possible that anyone else would have visited the cottage, but perhaps after all he was being precipitate. With straining eyes he stared out over the faintly luminous water, clinging to hope. Five minutes passed, ten minutes. No, he was deluding himself, and losing precious time. If Kathryn had been coming, she'd have been on her way by now. . . . Suddenly the cottage door opened and he saw her shadowy figure emerge and the beam of a torch being directed at her. That settled it!

With a heavy heart he made his way to the patch of gravel and re-entered the water. The shock of failure had exhausted him more than all his earlier efforts and his arms and legs felt leaden. For a moment he thought seriously of suicide as a solution of his problem, and wondered what it would feel like to drown. If he swam out into deep water and let himself sink the police might never discover the truth and they certainly wouldn't be able to prove anything against Kathryn. Then he remembered that bodies floated after a few days, and anyway he doubted if he had the strength to reach deep water. He'd merely be found in the morning after the tide had gone out, lying on the mud.

He swam on with flagging strokes. The ebb had set in now, and out here in midstream he could barely hold his own against the tide. He changed to an over-arm stroke, battling with his tiredness. The sooner he was across, the sooner he could rest.

He still had half the distance to cover when, out of the darkness ahead of him, a solid object suddenly loomed. At first he thought it was a barrel or a piece of wreckage floating down on the ebb, but as he swam closer he saw that it was a boat. An old derelict dinghy! Even then, because it was drifting back towards the cottage, it didn't occur to him that this could be *his* dinghy. Only when he

98

grabbed the deeply laden stern and peered in and touched the jerrycans did the full extent of his good fortune come home to him.

His joy then was so great that it was all he could do not to shout aloud. He realised at once that Kathryn must have pushed the boat out into the blue to prevent the police finding it—and that meant that they were still safe. He needn't run away—he could go back to the island and carry on as they had planned. This, surely, was what a reprieve would have felt like. It was life!

With returning hope came new vigour. Hoisting himself over the stern, he found an oar and began to scull himself back across the creek. The main thing now was to get the dinghy behind the screen of the island sea-wall before the tide went down. There was, he remembered, a breach in the wall somewhere, and if he could find it quickly he might still have time to float the boat in. Otherwise he would have no alternative but to manhandle both it and its contents up the mud, and that would mean leaving a trail behind him.

He hadn't gone very far before a dip in the bank and a rush of pent-up water into the creek told him that he had reached the spot. Half sculling, half pushing against the bottom, he managed by slow degrees to manœuvre the dinghy into the turbulent channel. He held it there for a while, jammed against the mud with an oar while he gathered his strength. Then, with a powerful shove or two, he forced it round behind the wall into a quiet rill. Sweating and trembling from the fierce exertion, he sat down on the gunwale to recover.

It was too dark to unload the boat with safety—that would have to wait until morning—but at least he could slake his thirst and take the edge off his hunger. He felt about in the bottom until he found a tin mug, and carefully poured out a ration of water. Petrol-flavoured though it was, it tasted better than any drink he could remember. He found some biscuits too, and chewed them slowly, making the most of them. It might be a long while before he could afford to eat his fill again.

He still felt jubilant at the dramatic turn of events, but as he came to consider the position more calmly he realised that in fact the immediate crisis was by no means over.

It had been an amazing stroke of luck to run into the dinghy like that, and all his wants were now supplied, but Kathryn wouldn't know that he'd intercepted it and she must be almost off her head with worry. Tomorrow her anxiety would be sharper still and by the next day, if he knew her, she'd be so desperate on his account that she'd probably do something rash. In one way or another, he'd got to let her know that the dinghy had arrived.

He munched another biscuit and turned the problem over in his mind. An idea slowly matured—there was, he thought, a way, provided he was prepared to accept a slight risk. But he couldn't do anything about it tonight—the creek was already showing a rim of steep bare mud at its edges and before long it would be dry. If he made any move now it would be the same old story—he would leave tracks in the smooth surface that would point like a sign-post to his hiding-place. Nor could he attempt anything in daylight. He would have to wait until high water to-morrow night, and trust that Kathryn would leave the initiative to him.

He was just finishing his frugal meal when a glow in the sky over in the direction of the cottage drew him to the top of the sea-wall again. This time, he saw, there were two cars approaching along the causeway. Kathryn was evidently in for a gruelling night. He watched them draw up, and saw the cottage door open and someone go in. He continued to watch, wishing he could help her, trying with all his might to communicate with her, to buoy her strength up with his own. Not until the visit was over and the second car had left and darkness had fallen once more on the house did he feel free to unroll his sleeping-bag. By that time he was so dazed with tiredness that sleep came almost as he lay down.

He woke at daybreak, wonderfully refreshed. The ground had been more restful than his prison bed and for almost the first time since the trial his sleep had been undisturbed by ugly dreams. He lay for a while in a state of almost complete physical contentment, lazily watching a wheeling gull, sniffing the tangy air, listening to the soothing trickle of water and the gentle hiss of mud. The wide sky above him was a pale, clear blue; the sun was just coming up over the sea-wall. The day promised to be exquisite—

the sort to make the blood tingle. It seemed too fantastic to think that in an hour or two from now they had intended to take him out and hang him in a prison courtyard and bury him in quicklime in a nameless grave.

All the same, the grim thought brought him back to realities. He slid quickly from his bag and put on his khaki shorts and shirt and sea-boots. Then he took the binoculars from the dinghy and climbed cautiously up the sloping wall until he had a clear but safe view of the cottage between tufts of stiff sea-grass. The place looked so near through the glasses that he felt he could touch it if he stretched out his hand. He could make out the features of a man apparently dozing behind the wheel of a car, but there was no sign of life anywhere else. Kathryn wasn't stirring yet. Judging by the position of the sun, the time must be about half past six. The tide was right out. All around was yellow-gleaming mud and the grey-green grass of the saltings. Not everyone's idea of heaven, perhaps, but Charles thought at that moment that he had rarely seen anything so peaceful and lovely.

He turned and surveyed his own domain. The island was four or five acres in extent and completely flat inside the wall except for the odd hummock here and there. At some time an attempt must have been made to reclaim and cultivate it, for it was impossible otherwise to account for the wall. Perhaps Creek Cottage had once housed the hopeful farmer! But that must have been scores of years ago, and with the breaching of the wall the place had long since reverted to its natural state. The whole area was now a maze of muddy rills and creeks and little pools, separated from each other by islands and peninsulas of coarse grass. Wherever there was grass there was sea-lavender—tall mauve sprays in full flower, deliciously scenting the air. At this state of the tide it was like some wonderful wild garden. At high water, of course, everything but the hummocks would be covered and the island inside the wall would become, if only for a few minutes, a lagoon.

Rather reluctantly he got down from his perch and started out to explore his kingdom. He felt extremely hungry, but he was anxious to find out whether it was safe for him to move about on the island in daylight and the best time to experiment was before the cottage came to life.

He began to make a circuit round the inside of the wall, stopping every few yards to see if anything of the mainland was visible. The walk reassured him. Even at the point most distant from the land—even though he climbed a foot or two up the wall—he could still see nothing but the sky. And that meant that no one could see him. As long as he was careful about the break in the wall he could move freely and without worry at all times. That would certainly make life much pleasanter.

He picked his steps with care through the flotsam that the tide had deposited under the wall—small bits of driftwood and several quite large planks, a huge rope fend-off torn from some wharf, a tattered yachting cap, a motor tyre and innumerable bottles and old sharp tins that people had thrown away after picnics. A ball of tarred twine caught his eye and he gathered it up and stuffed it into his pocket. He might have a use for it later on.

When he had completed his tour of the wall he set to work to explore the open centre. The time might come when it would be necessary for him to move quickly over this ground, and he must know it thoroughly. For half an hour he walked backwards and forwards over the hummocks, studying the pattern of the rills and creeks. Then he returned to the dinghy.

By now he was ravenous, and as he regarded his store of tins he felt it would be no great effort to consume the whole lot in a day. Obviously he'd have to cut down on exercise and husband his energies. He opened one of the tins of guavas and ate two of the fruits, followed them with a piece of meat roll and a few biscuits. He wondered if he dared make a small fire of dry sticks and brew some tea in a mug, but decided not to risk it at the moment and contented himself with water. He counted the cigarettes and smoked one of them with slow relish, blessing Kathryn for her forethought. She'd done a splendid job with the dinghy. If only she could know—if only she could see him now! Still, by this time tomorrow she'd be out of her misery.

While he smoked he watched the antics of little green crabs as they scuttled about in a reed-encircled pool of mud and water that lay just beyond the boat. Occasionally two of them would converge and rear up on their back legs and fight, their armoured claws clashing noisily. Then one would turn and run and at the first chance wriggle and slither its way down into the brown ooze until nothing of it showed above the surface but its bright beady eyes. There were moments of quiet when the pool seemed devoid of life, yet when he looked closely Charles could count a dozen pairs of eyes. It was a pity, he thought, that the things weren't edible. If he were reduced to living off the country, his diet, as far as he could see, would consist of sea-kale.

Presently he stubbed out his cigarette butt and thrust it deep into a crack in the rock-hard earth at the foot of the wall. Then he turned his attention to the disposal of the stores. It was important, he felt, to keep them hidden away, so that if by any chance the police did decide to take a look at the islands they wouldn't at once find conclusive evidence of his presence there. The likelihood that he would be able to give them the slip in such an eventuality was small, but if they found his gear scattered about the place it would be nil.

During his walk he had discovered three convenient mud-holes half buried in sea-lavender and in these he now concealed everything he had. The two jerrycans went into one hole, the tinned food into the second, and all the rest of the stuff, tightly wrapped in the tarpaulin, into the third. By the time he had drawn the sea-lavender around them again there was nothing to catch the casual eye and he felt confident that only a thorough combing of the place would uncover them. With these caches established, his freedom of action was to some extent restored.

It wasn't so easy to decide what to do about the dinghy. The boat was too big to be effectively camouflaged; anyone who so much as set foot on the sea-wall would spot it at once. At the same time, he couldn't set it adrift again—quite apart from the risk, he would probably need it later on. He puzzled over the problem for a long while, and in the end he devised a plan. Lower down the creek there was a small creek he knew of, a shallow saucer in the mud which never quite dried out even at low-water springs. He and Kathryn had sometimes used it as an anchorage for *Spray*. On the next night tide, he decided, he would row the boat to the pool and sink it there. He would have to swim back, but the distance wasn't too great. Then in an emergency he could recover it at any low water by walking through the mud to the pool and dragging it out.

Satisfied that he had taken all the precautions possible at the moment, he climbed again to his look-out on the sea-wall and settled down with the glasses. The position gave him a commanding view all round the compass. Looking northwards, he could see the main channel of the Medway, with the great new oil refinery on the Isle of Grain beyond it. To the east, he could just make out the superstructure of the old warships that were kept moored in Stangate Creek. On the landward side there was Lower Halstow with its rifle range and factory chimney and, a little farther away, the village of Upchurch where a woman was wheeling a bicycle down a garden path and an energetic farmer was already at work with a tractor. He could see right along the creek to the spot where Kathryn had dropped him the previous evening. The whole string of islands between Twinney and the main river lay open to his inspection. He had no defences if his whereabouts should be discovered, but at least not much could happen in this southern bulge of the estuary without his knowing about it.

With that consoling thought he turned his glasses on to the cottage again and quietly awaited developments.

CHAPTER IV

Kathryn's emotional collapse hadn't lasted long. In a very short time she had taken a fresh grip of herself and gone up to bed—not to sleep, but to think. The position was about as bad as it could be, but Charles needed her help more than ever now and she'd simply got to discover some way out.

She was still worried by the possibility that the loaded dinghy might be found but there was nothing whatever she could do about that and in any case it might not happen for days. The immediate and vital problem was obviously how to get a new lot of supplies to the island.

One thing was clear—she couldn't do anything while the police were watching her and she couldn't hope to detach herself from them as long as she stayed at the cottage. What, she wondered, were her chances of doing so if she left the cottage? Presumably they would follow her, and they must be expert at shadowing people. All the same, she believed she might be able to elude them. She imagined herself slipping in and out of cloakrooms, dashing into lifts at the last moment, driving up to town and mixing with the rush-hour crowds. There must be all sorts of ways.

Even if she succeeded in shaking them off, though, it was still going to be difficult to get anything to the island. A boat of some sort was essential, but she had no dinghy any more and she doubted if she could manage *Spray* single-handed. Of course, there was always Peter's dinghy. . . .

Once she had thought of that, a plan began to take shape in her mind. Suppose she went off in the car early in the morning on a shopping expedition and bought a few stores, ostensibly for herself, and then somehow contrived to give her police escort the slip. She could spend the day in some

place where she wouldn't be recognised—a cinema, perhaps—and after dark she could make her way to Upnor,
the little Medway village just below Rochester where Peter
kept *Witch*. Peter was on holiday in Corsica, so the boat
was bound to be there and the dinghy would be drawn up
on the foreshore as it always was. She could row to the
island at night and leave the stores and row back again. . . .

For a time, because the situation was so desperate that no
plan seemed too fantastic, she almost believed in the possibility of such cloak-and-dagger stuff. After a while,
though, common sense reasserted itself. She wasn't
physically equipped for that sort of enterprise—she doubted
if she *could* row six miles out and six miles back in a single
night, and anyhow she'd probably lose her way in the darkness and everything would go wrong. Besides, now she
came to think of it there wouldn't be any oars in Peter's
dinghy, because no one ever left oars lying around, and
she didn't see how she could get hold of any without
drawing attention to herself. It simply wasn't her sort of
plan.

For that matter, eluding the police wasn't very sensible,
either—in fact, it was the very thing she ought to avoid.
Once she deliberately gave them the slip their suspicions
would become certainties and they wouldn't rest until they
found out what she'd been doing. Her aim ought to be
the exact opposite—to dispel suspicion by keeping close to
them all the time.

That line of thought suggested a more subtle approach.
Suppose she bought some stores and put them in the
cottage—just a few, not enough to excite interest—and then
went away? The police would follow her. Charles would
see them depart, and when all was quiet he could swim
ashore and help himself.

For a moment she believed she had hit upon the solution.
Then she realised that the police might still leave someone
to keep an eye on the cottage, in which case the practical
effect of her going would be the desertion of Charles.
And she wouldn't even know what was happening. She
couldn't risk it—she'd got to make quite certain that the
supplies actually reached him. But how, unless she delivered them herself?

At that point, she had a new idea. Boldness might be

the best answer to the problem—sheer brazen nerve. The police were obviously hoping that she'd do something clandestine—that was what they were waiting for. They'd never expect her to take supplies out under their very noses! Now wasn't there some way in which she could do that?

She believed there was. Suppose she told Sergeant Fellowes in the morning that she felt like having a sail in *Spray* and asked him to join her in a picnic lunch on board? She'd be able to manage the boat with his help and he'd almost certainly agree to come if she told him she'd made up her mind to go, because it was his job not to lose sight of her. They could sail out past Twinney Island in full view of Charles and at a suitable moment she could send the sergeant forward to do some little thing in the bows and while he was busy she could drop some food over the stern. Even if it were only a couple of tins and a bottle of beer it would give Charles something to be going on with. The things would sink, and he could recover them from the mud after dark.

The idea seemed so simple and so practicable that Kathryn relaxed for a moment, and promptly fell asleep.

As soon as she woke next morning, anxiety came flooding back. Crossing to the window she stood motionless with her eyes focused on Twinney Island, as though by concentrating she could pierce the barrier of the sea-wall and discover how Charles was faring. The place appeared as deserted as it had always been, but she lifted her hand in salutation in case he should be watching her. Then her thoughts turned again to the scheme she had evolved the night before. It still seemed sound in principle—the trouble was that at best it would supply only a fraction of his needs. And there were hazards. Suppose by some awful mischance the sergeant were to notice her dropping the things overboard!

Suddenly, as she gazed out over the green, attractive archipelago, a much better idea suggested itself. Instead of having lunch aboard *Spray*, why shouldn't she and the sergeant have it on one of the islands? Not Twinney, of course, but perhaps the one next to it. She would pack the food in the big rucksack, with some extra tins in the bottom, and the sergeant could carry it ashore himself. As her guest, he would hardly show curiosity about the contents. She would scatter the things around, while they ate as people always did at picnics, and when the time came to clear up it would be the easiest thing in the world to stuff a few tins down into the long grass when he wasn't looking. There would be no risk and if the plan worked she could try the same thing again another day. Charles would be certain to realise the point of it all, and he'd swim over after dark and collect what had been left for him. It was beautifully straightforward and absolutely foolproof.

Then she remembered the tides. High water would be around eleven o'clock and that meant that by the time lunch was over the ebb would be so far advanced that it would be too late to get *Spray* back across the creek. The plan would work all right tomorrow, when the tide would be nearly an hour later, but not today.

Once again her troubled gaze swept the sea wall. By tomorrow night Charles wouldn't have eaten or drunk for nearly sixty hours. How long could a man go without water? Suppose he fell ill?—suppose he hadn't the strength left to swim?

Still, worrying wouldn't help. As she dressed, she forced herself to concentrate on improvements to her plan rather than on Charles's plight. There was, she remembered, an old coat of his aboard *Spray*—she could take that ashore for them to sit on and with a bit of luck she might be able to leave it behind as well. Other things, too—a tin opener, cigarettes, matches. Anything that could be easily hidden. . . .

At that moment she heard the noise of car engines outside the cottage and hurried downstairs. The constable was just driving off along the causeway and she saw with satisfaction that Sergeant Fellowes had taken his place. He turned at the sound of her step and gave her a slightly sheepish "Good morning."

Without difficulty she conjured up a look of agitation. "Is there any news, Sergeant?"

"No, miss, he's still at large."

"Thank God," she said, and went in to make tea.

Half an hour later she set out to do her shopping. Sergeant Fellowes raised no objection when she told him where she was going—she was quite free, he said, to go anywhere she pleased provided she didn't mind him coming too. His manner towards her was a curious mixture of deference to a celebrity, obvious admiration of her good looks, and embarrassment that it had fallen to his lot to keep an official eye on her. On the whole, she found his attitude promising.

As soon as she reached Rochester she parked the car, bought an armful of newspapers, and sat down on a public bench to read them.

The first one she picked up turned out to be typical of all. There was a huge photograph of Charles, and underneath in bold letters the words "Have YOU Seen This Man?" There was an account of his escape in his underclothes and an interview with a woman who now remembered seeing him running along a road near the prison. There was a story about the close watch that was being kept on the ports and the unlikelihood that Hilary could already have left the country. The crime reporter, in his own analysis of the situation, recalled that Hilary had been something of a yachtsman and referred to the possibility that he might attempt to get away in his own boat. A crisp paragraph recorded the fact that Miss Kathryn Forrester had left her flat in Chelsea and that her present whereabouts was unknown. Inset was a photograph of Kathryn. The facts of Louise Hilary's murder and of the trial were summarised in a small "box". All the rest of the front page was taken up with pictures and descriptions of the ghastly fire at the prison.

The other papers had covered the same ground under their own staring headlines. "Hilary Cheats Gallows." "Where is Charles Hilary?" "Yard Leads Nation-wide Manhunt." "Keep Your Eyes Open!"

For a while, Kathryn sat appalled. Only now did she realise fully what Charles and she were up against. In a few hours, the pack would be baying along every trail. It was horrible.

She felt slightly sick and suddenly remembered that she hadn't eaten for nearly twenty-four hours. It wouldn't help Charles for her to go hungry. She found a restaurant and had a light meal, ignoring the pointed interest of the waitresses.

Afterwards she did her shopping, laying in tinned meat

and ham and cheese, biscuits and fruit, a couple of loaves, milk and beer. Considering that she was proposing to offer hospitality to the sergeant, her purchases didn't strike her as excessive. She also bought a few household and toilet things that she would need at the cottage.

She felt rather surprised, as she walked from shop to shop, that she couldn't see anything of Fellowes, particularly after what he'd said about keeping close to her. It looked, after all, as though she wouldn't have had much difficulty in slipping away if she'd wanted to—unless, of course, the sergeant wasn't the only man on the job. The streets were fairly busy, and it was hard to be sure. It occurred to her that perhaps some woman was trailing her. Anyhow, it didn't matter now, and the more unconcerned she appeared the better. She completed her purchases and returned to the car park.

Fellowes was waiting for her there and as she approached he opened the door of her car almost as though he were her chauffeur. She saw him eyeing the shopping basket, and forced a smile.

"You're wasting your time, Sergeant," she said, "but have a look by all means." She let him put the basket in the back seat for her. "The beer, by the way, is for you."

It became clear as they turned on to the causeway that something was afoot at the cottage. Three or four cars were parked in a line near the shingle and there was a knot of men waiting beside the door. For a horrible moment Kathryn thought that this was the beginning of a search party, but as she drew nearer she saw that several of the men had cameras, and realised that they were all from the Press.

As soon as she got out of the car the reporters clustered round her and began to fire their questions. Sergeant Fellowes looked as though he would be happy to intervene if they got too rough but this was a situation that Kathryn was well able to handle. It was even possible, she thought, that she might be able to turn it to good account. She appeared reluctant to talk, said the only reason she had come to the cottage was to be alone and that she had no idea where Charles was, and altogether managed to give the impression of a woman distracted by worry. The photographers took pictures of the cottage, and the boat, and herself, and Sergeant Fellowes with his car, and when there was nothing else to take but mud and water and the reporters had extracted answers to all their questions, everyone departed with much slamming of doors.

The rest of the morning passed quietly. Just before one o'clock Kathryn asked the sergeant's permission to switch on the radio in his car in case there should be any fresh news, and once again she showed appropriate relief when the announcer said that Hilary was still missing. Then she prepared some sandwiches and opened a bottle of beer and joined Fellowes in a small patch of shade at the back of the cottage where they could eat and drink without tantalising Charles.

Presently she began to talk in a nostalgic way about *Spray* and the good times she had had aboard her in the past and the pleasures of sailing in the estuary and around the islands. The sergeant, it appeared, knew little about the pastime at first hand but he was obviously interested, and when she admitted that she wasn't really skilful enough to sail the boat without a man's help she thought she detected a responsive gleam in his eye. He was definitely getting adjusted to his assignment and she didn't foresee the least difficulty in persuading him to come out with her next day. She felt a little conscience-stricken at having to make him a party to her plot, but she was hardly in a position to afford the luxury of scruples.

After lunch she decided to give a touch of varnish to some of *Spray's* bare patches, feeling that signs of activity around the boat at such a time would be an indication to Charles that she had a plan, and an encouragement to him. When she needed fresh water to wash the salt crust off the woodwork, Fellowes volunteered to take the pail to the well and fill it for her. Afterwards, as she poured varnish into an old tin that she had picked out from the debris at the edge of the mud, he looked as though he would have liked nothing better than to take a brush himself but wasn't sure whether painting a boat was quite the thing to be found doing if the inspector should call. Perhaps it would be carrying fraternisation a bit too far. In the end, he just sat on the shingle and watched.

Some more reporters came down in the late afternoon but they brought no fresh news and took none away.

About eight in the evening Fellowes was relieved by a constable whom Kathryn hadn't seen before. He was a stolid, middle-aged, moustached man named Skelton and his attitude was very official and correct. He kept walking up and down the causeway as though he were still on a beat, and at last his monotonous tread got on her nerves. She decided to go to bed and try to get some rest.

In fact, she slept badly again. The thought of Charles, so near, so lonely and so wretched, was an ache that never left her. With darkness, too, came new fears—that some less amenable person than Fellowes might turn up in the morning, that the weather might suddenly deteriorate. . . .

That anxiety, at least, proved unfounded. When she put her head out of the window soon after daybreak she saw that the sky was clear and the outlook most promising. She would get her sail all right. The light southerly breeze was perfect.

She stood for a moment looking out over the mud. By now every detail of the scene was only too familiar. Her gaze took in the island, and the boat, and the complex pattern of footmarks between *Spray* and the shore that she and the police had made, and the line of flotsam brought in by the night tide. Suddenly she frowned.

It *couldn't be*!—she must be imagining things.

Flinging on her clothes, she raced downstairs. Outside the door she pulled up and nodded casually to the constable, trying to give the impression that she was merely taking the morning air. But her eyes swivelled to the object she had seen from the upper room, and she knew she had been right.

It was an opened tin, held in the mud by its sharp round lid. A tin of Trinidad guavas!

CHAPTER V

For a second or two she continued to stare at it, hardly able to believe that the miracle had happened. Yet the evidence was conclusive. It couldn't just be an old tin that had been washed in during the night—it didn't look old, and it didn't look as though it had been washed in. The way the sharp edge had been pressed into the mud was a clear sign of human agency—and there was only one possible explanation. Charles had found the dinghy, and this was his way of telling her. He must have swum in on the night tide and pushed the tin down through the water.

Her relief was unbounded, for at one stroke her two most pressing anxieties had been lifted. Charles had everything he needed for the time being, and his morale was obviously high. Not only that, but he'd presumably got the dinghy with him on the island, so she needn't torment herself any longer with the fear that it might be picked up. The imminent dangers had all passed. For the first time since his escape, they had a breathing space.

She glanced back at the police car. The constable had disappeared round the corner of the house—probably he was off on his beat again! She walked along the edge of the mud and dislodged the tin with her foot. Then, making sure she was still unobserved, she ripped off the coloured wrapper and stuffed it deep in the grass that lined the shore. For a moment she gazed out towards the island; then turned and made her way nonchalantly back to the cottage. The incident was over—the evidence was destroyed.

She felt glad now that she had said nothing definite to Sergeant Fellowes about going out in *Spray*. Her plan might come in useful at a later stage if it became necessary to augment Charles's supplies, but for the moment she was content to leave well alone. She would do better to concentrate on disarming the suspicions of the police.

Immediately after breakfast she drove into Rochester again and bought another stack of papers. The headlines, though almost as large as on the previous day, had lost some of their punch, and most of the stories consisted of reporters' theories. Less was being said now about the possibility of Charles leaving the country by yacht, presumably because the newspapermen had found *Spray* at the cottage and no boats had been reported missing. Several of the papers mentioned that Inspector Bates was still directing his inquiries in the Medway district, but no details were given. The police were evidently being rather secretive about the progress of the manhunt. A complication, according to one report, was that the Yard was being inundated by circumstantial stories that a man answering to Hilary's description had been seen in places as far apart as Tunbridge Wells and Stockton-on-Tees!

On the whole, Kathryn found the news reassuring—whatever the police were up to, they were certainly not on the right scent. She did her routine shopping and lunched in Rochester and in the afternoon she and Sergeant Fellowes had a look over the Castle. She had rarely felt less like sight-seeing, but it seemed better than haunting the creek all the time.

When she returned to the cottage in the early evening, the reporters were waiting for her again. There was a repetitiveness about their questions that disturbed her; it was as though they didn't believe what she'd already told them. After a few minutes she announced firmly that she had nothing more to say and went into the house. Even then they didn't leave immediately, and at seven o'clock one of them was still sitting in his car at the landward end of the causeway, watching the cottage. It was bad enough, she thought, to have the police at her heels the whole time without being shadowed by inquisitive newspapermen as well.

She had just come to the conclusion that it might be a good idea if she left the district for a day or two when Inspector Bates appeared. One glance at his face told her that something unpleasant was in store. His expression was grim, his manner no longer touched with sympathy Abruptly, he came to the point.

"Miss Forrester, I understand that you accepted a transferred charge telephone call at your flat last Thursday afternoon?"

So that was it! And to think she had been feeling almost complacent that morning!

"Why, yes," she said, struggling to keep the fear out of her voice.

"At about half past four?"

"About then."

"Who was it from?"

"The operator said it was from my brother—that was why I took it."

"And was it?"

"I don't know. The girl told me to go ahead but nothing happened. I said 'Hallo' once or twice but when no one answered I hung up."

"The operator says she connected you."

"She may have done, but I didn't hear anyone. You know what telephones are like."

"Did you complain to the operator?"

"No."

"Did you try to get in touch with your brother afterwards and find out what it was all about?"

"No—I'd already decided to come down here and as I told you I didn't want to see anyone—not even John."

"Didn't you think it rather strange that he should make a transferred charge call?"

"I didn't think about it at all."

"Have you written to him or telephoned him since?"

"No, I've had too much on my mind."

"That I can believe," said Bates dryly. "Miss Forrester, would it surprise you to learn that that telephone call was made from a box very close to Pentonhurst Prison a few minutes after Charles Hilary escaped?"

Kathryn gave him a startled look. "I never thought of that. . . ." She broke off and seemed to consider the idea. "Yes, I suppose it could have been Charles," she agreed after a moment. "And that would account for my not hearing anything—he must have been interrupted . . . Oh, God!"

"You still insist that you didn't speak to him?"

"I certainly didn't speak to him." She was beginning to feel a little more confident now—if the operator hadn't actually heard them talking to each other, she might still be able to lie her way out.

Bates grunted. "Well, we'll leave that for the time being. Now I'd like to ask you a few questions about your journey down here that afternoon. I understand you stopped at a garage for petrol and while you were there you had a conversation with an A.A. scout."

"Yes," said Kathryn, suddenly tense again.

"He and I had quite a long chat about you this morning. I made a point of asking him whether you appeared to be in reasonably good spirits when he talked to you, and he said he thought you were. It seems you even managed to smile at him."

"Is that so extraordinary?"

"Considering that Charles Hilary was going to be hanged at eight o'clock the next morning, I think it is—*most* extraordinary." The inspector paused significantly, while Kathryn inwardly cursed her folly. "Of course," he continued after a moment, "if when you talked to him you knew that Hilary was safely hidden away in the back of your car it would have been rather a different matter. . . ."

"That's nonsense, Inspector. Good heavens, the A.A. man would have seen him."

"Didn't you have a rug?"

"There was nothing under the rug."

"I wish I could believe you. Unfortunately you've given me every reason to distrust you."

"I don't see that I have."

"When I saw you last you gave me to understand that you and Hilary didn't own a dinghy. Do you remember?"

"Yes . . ."

"Well, I've been making some inquiries at the yacht club up the river. It may interest you to know that three people can remember you having a dinghy. I'm told that it had the words 'Tender to *Spray*' painted in white letters on the back. . . ." He paused invitingly. "Well—what have you to say?"

Kathryn had gone very white. "Oh, *that* one," she said. "That was a long while ago. I'd almost forgotten it."

"Not so long ago, Miss Forrester. In May, to be exact. You were seen in the third week of May towing it behind your boat *Spray*."

She was silent.

"Why did you tell me that you hadn't a dinghy? Why did you say that your boat didn't need one?"

"I—I don't know. I was upset."

"That's no answer at all." The inspector's tone became sharper. "Let me tell you what I think about all this. I think that the transferred charge call was from Hilary, and that you spoke to him, and that you arranged to pick, him up. I think you brought him down here in your car and that he went off in the dinghy. That's why his boots were missing, that's why there was only one sleeping-bag, that's why there was no sign of his clothes. You helped him, and that's why your own boots were wet. Well, Miss Forrester, that's true, isn't it? He went away in the dinghy."

"No," she said faintly. "It's not true, I haven't seen him."

"Then why did you lie about the dinghy?"

"Because I was afraid. When you came down here and asked me about it I realised that I hadn't seen it and I thought—I thought perhaps he might have got here before me and gone off in it. Afterwards, when I had the chance, I looked to see if there were any footmarks in the mud but there weren't except those that your policeman had made so I knew I'd lied for nothing, but it seemed too late then to tell the truth. I'm sure what really happened is that someone stole the dinghy during the summer when we were away for so long. Anyhow, it's ridiculous—where would he go in a dinghy? It was a tiny thing—he couldn't get far."

Bates looked out across the mud flats. "No," he said thoughtfully, "he couldn't get far. He'd hardly have gone out to sea in it. But he might have taken it to one of those islands out there, full of provisions, mightn't he? He might be there now."

"I'm sure he isn't."

"We shall see." Bates moved towards the door. "Frankly, Miss Forrester, I don't believe a single word you've told me. I'm certain you know where he is, and I think that by this time tomorrow we shall have him in our hands. Good night."

CHAPTER VI

On the island, time had slipped by with surprising speed and up to now Charles had not known a moment of tedium. The freedom of the life was in itself an almost sensual pleasure. To be able to roam at will over five acres, to lie in the sun, to watch the flow and ebb of the tide, to swim at high water in his own private and secluded swimming pool, to prepare his simple meals—these all seemed to him idyllic pursuits after the horrors of prison. Every passing hour had brought an increased feeling of security. He had known only one moment of alarm, when during a midday repast his presence had attracted the attention of a great flock of seagulls. They had wheeled and screeched overhead until he had feared that someone ashore might wonder what all the fuss was about, but in the end they had departed and not come back.

Visual reconnaissance had been one of his chief occupations and a great help in keeping loneliness at bay. Through the glasses he had been able to study the changing expressions on Kathryn's face and often to read her thoughts. What had happened ashore had been very much in accordance with his expectations. The close guard on the cottage and the descent of the newspapermen had been inevitable. He had assumed that Kathryn's ostentatious activity on *Spray* must be connected in some way with a plan for getting supplies to him, but it hadn't worried him because if all went well she should know the truth about the dinghy before she could attempt any kind of relief expedition. He had felt a little anxiety in case she failed to notice the guava tin, but that had been dispelled by events. He had watched the arrival and departure of Inspector Bates without sensing any imminent threat. With luck, he thought, these police attentions would die down in a few days and then he and Kathryn could make contact again. He spent a good deal of time pondering the next step.

On the morning after the inspector's visit there was a slight heat haze and by the time he was able to see the cottage clearly from the island Kathryn had gone off in her car with her police escort and the place was deserted. Charles took the opportunity to light a small fire and cook himself a hot breakfast, not forgetting afterwards to bury every trace of ash. He had got into the way of regarding low water, with its formidable barrier of mud, as a comparatively safe period, and it was not until the tide began to flow at about eleven that he mounted to his observation post to keep continuous watch. By then the day was brilliant, and though the creeping tide was brown at its tip with scum and bubbles, over by the pool where he had sunk the dinghy its surface had a diamond sparkle. Serene and contented as a man could be whose life was legally forfeit, he watched the channels deepen and the leaf-vein rills begin to fill

It was with Kathryn's return that he felt the first pang of uneasiness. As she got out of the car he saw that her face had the set, preoccupied look of someone who was deeply worried, and he missed the quick glance of reassurance that she always threw in his direction. She was carrying a large paper bag in addition to her shopping basket, and she disappeared at once into the house.

When she emerged a few minutes later, he had a shock. She was wearing a frock he had never seen before—a tasteless, garish thing of pillar-box red. It was so unlike her to buy new clothes in a hurry, and such clothes, and at such a time, that he hadn't the least doubt it was intended as a signal. Some danger threatened, some danger of which he must be warned. There was only one serious danger that Charles could think of. The police must be going to search the islands after all, and presumably on this tide.

He fought down the sudden fear that set his heart pounding and made him want to yawn his head off, and tried to consider what he should do. If they were going to comb the islands he would be much better off on the mainland, but any attempt to get there before high water would mean leaving tracks in the mud which would tell the whole story. On the other hand, if he waited until high water the police would be upon him, and it would probably be too late. There was just a chance, perhaps, that he might be able to give them the slip as they approached—hide on the side of the island away from them and slide quietly into the full creek and swim away unobserved either to an island they had already searched or to the mainland. Much would depend on how many of them there were and on how they disposed their forces. At best, the attempt would be frightfully hazardous.

The only other possibility was to try to camouflage himself with grass and sea-lavender here on the island. There was no place of certain concealment, but if he lay lengthwise on the mud in one of the narrow rills and pulled the vegetation over him he might escape detection provided the search were not too thorough.

He tried to put himself in the position of the police. The search party would undoubtedly come by water, and that meant they would come from the main river, out beyond the string of islands. There was no reason why they should want to search Twinney first—in fact they wouldn't be able to, because they could get into this creek only near the top of the tide. They would have to start at the other end of the chain and move in as the channels deepened. That being so, by the time they got to Twinney they would have searched in vain for several hours; they would be getting tired of scrambling across rills and falling into holes in the saltings and sliding about in the mud. At Twinney their search might well be perfunctory, particularly as the island had been under surveillance from the cottage for several days.

All the same, the thought of lying in the grass while searchers beat around him was a terrifying one. And he couldn't even be sure of being able to do that—if the police didn't arrive until the tide was at its height, the inside of the island would be a lake; and the sea-wall itself offered no protection. They would be bound to find him.

In the end he decided to wait and see what happened before making up his mind on a course of action. For the moment there was urgent work to be done—he must devise a more satisfactory method of hiding his gear. Arrangements that were proof against a casual glance, wouldn't suffice for a search.

The tins, already much reduced in number, presented no difficulty—he sank them in a muddy pool from which he could easily recover them if he survived. The jerrycans and other impedimenta were more of a problem. Using a piece of driftwood as a trowel he scooped a deep hole for them in the mud. It was a filthy and arduous job, but when he had finished there was space both for the cans and for the tarpaulin-wrapped bundle. Everything he possessed had gone into the bundle, even the binoculars. He flung the piece of wood in on top and shovelled the mud back with his hands and then smoothed the surface until it was indistinguishable from the rest of the pool.

Having disposed of his effects he climbed again to his look-out and gazed anxiously around. He felt somewhat handicapped without the glasses but his sight was keen and visibility was excellent along the chain of islands. He sat there for so long without seeing any unusual movement that he almost began to think he must have misinterpreted Kathryn's signal. The arrival of another police car and three reporters' cars at the cottage suddenly disabused him. There had been no mistake. The crowd was collecting for the kill!

Then, a mile or more away, he saw a dark figure outlined against the sky on the top of one of the islands—and another. They were coming, and from the main channel as he had expected. Presently they disappeared again, and after a few moments a boat nosed out from behind a promontory. It was a low, fast launch of shallow draught, and there were at least half a dozen men in it. Almost at once it shot between two more islands, and again there were moving figures on the skyline.

For half an hour Charles watched their progress, and the nearer they got the lower his spirits fell. They seemed to be searching very thoroughly indeed. Their technique on reaching each island was to drop one or two men and then swiftly encircle it before putting the rest ashore. Obviously the idea that their quarry might try to swim away had occurred to them—so that was ruled out. Once they had landed, they spread out and beat across each piece of ground in line abreast—tough, determined figures in sea-boots, with binoculars and sticks. And now Charles saw something else—they had a dog with them!

As the launch approached the island next to Twinney, he moved to another part of the wall to get a better view. They were so close now that he could recognise Inspector Bates and hear their voices clearly. He watched them land and begin to work their way forward. They were covering every yard, poking into rills and slashing at the long grass. The dog was dashing to and fro and nosing about everywhere. Suddenly Charles saw that he hadn't a chance. In ten minutes they would be on Twinney, and whatever he did they would find him

He gazed wildly around. His instinct, like that of any hunted animal, was to run—to swim away, make a dash for the mainland. But the crowd by the cottage had grown and they were all looking now in his direction. He'd be spotted at once.

He wondered how long he could swim under water. Not long enough to escape detection, he was sure. Suppose he got into the water with just his head showing? The tide was beginning to flow through the breach in the sea-wall, a racing stream, brown and turgid. If he got down into that stuff, would they notice his head? Would the dog find him? If only he could burrow like the crabs!

As the idea came to him, his skin crawled. It was so ghastly, so hideous in its possibilities that the very thought filled him with nausea—but was it any worse than being caught and dragged back to the scaffold? Could anything be worse than that?

The baying of the dog drove him into action. Stripping off his shorts and shirt he plunged them deep into the stream, with a stone on top to hold them down. Then he ran to the pool where he'd watched the crabs cavorting and thrust his arm into the reedy mud at its edge, testing the depth. The stuff was sloppy, like thick brown cream, but it seemed to have a firm bottom. He scooped up a double handful and smalmed it thickly over his face and hair, closing his eyes. Then, stark naked, he stepped into the pool and lay down full length in the liquid mud. Flat on his back, with his head almost touching the reeds and his feet out towards the centre, he began to work his body down into the ooze. At first he sank quickly, so that for a terrible moment he thought he was going down for good. But the mud, though soft, was nowhere deep and soon he felt it firm under his spine. It was very cold. He continued to wriggle, moving his buttocks, his shoulders, his neck and head. He felt the mud round his armpits, round his crutch. Little by little he was working his way down. A chill trickle ran over his stomach. His feet were under, his neck was under. He wondered if he would ever be able to get out again. The mud ran into his ears and the world became soundless. He was almost covered. He pushed his head down till only his eyes and mouth and nose were above the surface. There were only two things in his consciousness now. Death, and the sky above.

He knew almost nothing of what happened after that. No voice could reach him, and even if he had dared, it was impossible for him to turn his head. He guessed they were there all around him, but only for one instant did he know for certain—when his eyes, squinting out through half-shut, muddy lids, sensed a sea-boot in the grass beside him and he thought for a horrible moment it was going to step on him. But the shadow moved away, and all was stillness again. He didn't know whether they had gone or whether they were still combing the island. He was more frightened now of the mud than of the searchers—the mud, and the cramping cold. He lay motionless, fighting his panic. All sense of time had left him—he knew only that he must stick it to the limit of endurance.

That limit came sooner than he expected. Water suddenly ran into his eyes—dark muddy water that stung and half-blinded him. The tide had reached him! He must struggle out now even if he emerged at their very feet. He drew his arms back and clenched his fists and pressed downwards and forwards with his knuckles. His head came up an inch or two so that he could breathe again, but the suction of the mud held his body fast. He strained and twisted, trying to turn first to one side and then to the other, but he could get no grip on anything and he settled back in the same place. It was no use just struggling, he told himself—he must be slow and deliberate. For a few seconds he rested his aching muscles and then tried a different method, drawing his feet up until his knees broke the surface, and then pressing down against the firm bottom with his heels, trying to lever himself out head first. This time he made a little progress and he continued in the same way. Once or twice his feet slipped and shot forward and he lost much of what he'd gained, but he knew now that he could do it. The mud was getting softer and less tenacious as it absorbed the flowing water. Soon he felt the prick of grass under his neck and that encouraged him. He heaved and pushed with new vigour and his shoulders slowly emerged. He raised his buttocks and they came up with a great sucking plop. He gave a last shove with his heels and a moment later he was lying safe on the saltings.

Shakily he struggled to his knees. He was a hideously coated figure—an apparition to scare a man out of his wits if there had been any man to see. But there wasn't. As he clawed the mud from his face and opened his eyes he saw that he had the island to himself again. A wisp of blue smoke curled up from a cigarette butt at his feet, and that was all.

He shook some of the mud from his ears and wiped his hands on the grass, and climbed cautiously to the look-out. The police launch was tied up near the cottage and there were two groups of men standing in close knots beside the shingle. Kathryn was there, too, still in her red frock. She was talking to Bates.

Presently the groups broke up. Some of the men went to their cars, and five of the searchers got back into the launch. Its engine burst into life and with a roar and a fine bow wave it slipped past Twinney Island and disappeared in the distance. The last Charles heard of it was the barking of the dog.

Weary but triumphant, he dropped to the saltings again and lay down in the warm gently-flowing water and started to remove the traces of his ordeal.

CHAPTER VII

THE Assistant Commissioner pushed back his papers and looked up from his desk.

"All right, Inspector," he said briskly, "let's hear the details."

With an expression of deep gloom, Inspector Bates unrolled a large-scale map of the Medway district and spread it out on the A.C.'s table. If he wasn't exactly on the carpet, he was certainly on the defensive. He had felt so confident about his dinghy theory, so positive he would find Hilary, that he had pressed for and obtained permission to make that day's dispositions on the most elaborate scale. It was galling for him to have to admit that the whole ambitious manœuvre, with its unavoidable publicity, had been one of the biggest flops of his career—the more so because he still couldn't see where he had gone wrong. The fact that all his muscles ached abominably from the unaccustomed exercise on the saltings did nothing to improve his frame of mind.

"Well, sir," he said, "we carried out the search exactly as arranged. Three marine parties left Rochester just after dawn with instructions to look for the dinghy and any sign of Hilary. One of them went up river as far as the first lock. A second one covered the northern part of the estuary, from Rochester through Hoo and right along to Port Victoria and the river mouth." He indicated the places on the map. "The third—that was my party—covered this big southern loop. Between us we went over every inch of the estuary—every bit of marsh, every patch of saltings, every island."

"And there wasn't a trace?"

"Not a trace," said the inspector disgustedly.

"Too bad." The A.C. studied the map. "Could he

125

have hidden the dinghy at the water's edge, do you suppose, and made his way ashore when he saw you coming?"

Bates shook his head. "We took precautions against that. The local force had men out on foot and on bicycles and the whole shoreline was examined. There was no sign of the boat anywhere."

"You had a look at all the dinghies moored in the river, of course?"

"Yes, sir, *and* those drawn out at the yacht clubs and builders' yards. The boat's not in the Medway, that's certain."

"What about the Swale?" The Assistant Commissioner pointed to a wide tributary river that joined the Medway at Queenborough.

"Inspector Fuller handled that, on the same lines. All the Swale creeks, too. He found nothing."

"H'm. Well, what are the chances that Hilary might have slipped out to sea in this dinghy of his?"

"All the coastguards and signal stations were alerted the night he escaped, sir, and nothing unusual's been reported. I think he'd certainly have been spotted before he got far if he'd tried to put to sea in a cockleshell like that. Of course, there's always the possibility that he might have come to grief. . . ."

The A.C. gave a wry smile. "That would be very convenient, but we can hardly assume it without evidence. I should imagine something would have been washed ashore. Still, where *is* the boat? A dinghy loaded with supplies could hardly disappear overnight. I think we've got to face it, Inspector—it looks very much as though we've been on the wrong track."

Bates was grateful for the "we", but he felt reluctant to admit even collective error. "I could have sworn we should find him somewhere in the river, sir—everything pointed to it. It's as certain as anything can be that Hilary made that phone call—and having got through, would he be likely to break off without speaking? Besides, if the girl didn't pick him up, who did? And then there's her behaviour on the road, her lying about the dinghy, the sleeping-bag gone—everything fits. Absolutely everything."

"Except that the dinghy isn't in the river!"

"Yes," said Bates bitterly, "and that's something I just can't understand."

"Well, if it's not there," said the A.C., with a touch of irritation, "it's not there. Don't think I'm blaming you for organising that search, Inspector—you had a good lead and you were quite right to follow it. But we can't go on clinging to a theory if the facts don't support it. After all, the girl did have an answer to everything—she *may* be telling the truth. The dinghy might have been stolen during the summer as she suggested."

"I suppose so," Bates conceded. "I'm told dinghy thefts are fairly common. It could have been towed away and had its name painted out."

The A.C. nodded. "And if that *is* what happened, we've no solid grounds for believing that Hilary has been anywhere near the Medway at all?"

"No, sir."

"In fact, we can go further. If Hilary didn't take the dinghy with a full load of supplies that night, it's pretty certain he *hasn't* been there, because he'd have needed help and the girl hasn't given him any. Isn't that the position?"

"Yes, that's true enough," Bates admitted. "We've had her under surveillance day and night and she's made no attempt to communicate with him."

"Not even when you gave her a bit of rope that morning in Rochester?"

"No, sir, she didn't seem to notice. She certainly didn't make any move."

"What's her general attitude been like? Has she behaved like a woman who knew nothing?"

"Yes, I suppose she has," said Bates grudgingly. "She's been anxious for news, buying papers and listening to the radio, and looking very distressed. Of course, with her training I'd expect her to be able to put on a good act if she wanted to."

"Yes, that's a point." The A.C. was silent for a while, weighing up the position. "All the same, Inspector," he said at last, "considering how thin the evidence is I don't think we're right to concentrate on her the way we have been doing. I agree there's a suspicious chain of events but they've led us into a dead end. I suggest we give her a break for a few days—leave her alone and give her the feeling she's absolutely safe. Then we'll suddenly crack down again. If she does know where he is, we're much more likely to get results that way."

"Very well, sir."

"And meanwhile we'll switch the main effort to some of the other alternatives. If the girl isn't helping Hilary, someone else is, and we've got to find out who."

Bates looked glum. "We've checked up on all his friends and acquaintances, sir, and we've covered all his haunts. There's no indication of any other transferred charge call—no sign whatever that he got in touch with anyone but the girl that afternoon."

"Perhaps he didn't need to. Suppose he *did* speak to the girl, but merely asked her to get someone else to help him—someone they both knew? She might have rung the chap, and then shot off herself to the Medway to lead us away on a false scent."

"That's certainly a possibility," Bates agreed. "I must say I hadn't thought of it—I'll have a new check made right away. Otherwise, of course, our best hope is still that some member of the public will recognise him. By this time every man, woman and child in the country must know his features."

The A.C. glanced at the pile of letters on his desk. "That's not an unmixed blessing, Inspector," he said sourly.

"No, sir, but I think we're bound to get a line on him before long."

"We'd better!" said the A.C. "All right, Bates—keep in touch."

"I will, sir."

The inspector rolled up the map of the Medway with an air of finality and slipped an elastic band over it. At least, he thought, as he went stiffly out, he'd finished with those damned saltings!

CHAPTER VIII

KATHRYN had watched the methodical advance of the police launch upon Twinney Island with the despairing certainty that all was over. The search party was so large, the island so small. When, after a brief stay, they had come away without Charles, she had found it hard to adopt the calm "I-told-you-so" attitude that seemed called for. She couldn't begin to imagine by what magic of concealment he had succeeded in hiding even himself away—let alone the bulky dinghy!

But he *had* done so, and after the intolerable agony of the morning she felt almost light-headed with joy. Not only was he still free, but at a stroke his long-term prospects had been immeasurably improved. Safety—relative safety, at any rate—had been plucked from danger, for now that the police had searched the islands thoroughly they were hardly likely to go over the same ground again. Charles had won immunity for his hiding place.

For the first time since their parting under the sea wall, Kathryn could feel a reasonable hope that she would soon be able to see him again. But not yet!—first she must make absolutely certain that the cottage was no longer being watched and that she herself was free to move about without being followed. Both these things were more likely to happen, she decided, if she left the district as she had already half-planned to do, and went to some place where the innocence of her activities could be established beyond all question.

She had no difficulty in accounting for her proposed departure. In a brief interview with the crestfallen inspector, she said that she was tired of being badgered by newspapermen and that she intended to go into seclusion. Disarmingly she confided to Bates that she would be staying with her brother in Norwich and begged him not to disclose the fact to the Press! That night she drove to London.

Her stay in Norwich proved to be a stern exercise in self-discipline. It was even harder to keep away from the cottage than she had expected it would be. She missed the reassuring view of Twinney Island and the comforting sense of Charles's nearness, and although she kept telling herself that he had everything he needed for the time being and that no harm could possibly come to him, she couldn't help worrying, particularly at night. She tried to turn the sleepless hours to profit by considering some of the tasks that lay ahead. Often she found herself thinking about Louise Hilary and wondering if there weren't some way in which she could personally probe the dead woman's secret history. Only sheer physical prostration had prevented her from making the attempt after the trial, and it still seemed to be about the most hopeful line of inquiry.

Meanwhile, in case the police should still be watching her, she behaved all times in a determinedly unsuspicious manner. By day she stuck closely to her sister-in-law, Muriel, shopping with her and taking the children for walks and helping in the house. In the evenings she stayed indoors. Though she often longed to share her real troubles, she knew she must keep her own counsel about Charles, for his sake and for everyone else's. She continued, therefore, to play the part of a woman deeply anxious about the fate of her missing lover and totally ignorant of his whereabouts.

By the end of the third day she felt satisfied that her police escort had been withdrawn. She had kept a careful lookout during a trip to the sea in her car with the young Forrester family, and no one had followed them. By now the newspapers must know where she was, for people frequently recognised her in the streets and word would have got about, but she had no more trouble with reporters. The papers, having printed everything about the hunt that they could think of, were contenting themselves with brief daily paragraphs under some such headline as "Hilary Still Missing". The heat was off.

On the fourth day Kathryn returned to London. She did some shopping, and the same evening after dark she drove down to the Medway. Her plans were fluid. If by any chance the police were still hanging about the creek, she was prepared to walk round the sea-wall and swim out to the island as Charles had done on the night of his escape. If the police had gone, it would be a simple matter for him to join her at the cottage.

In fact the place appeared to be deserted when she pulled up by the shingle just after midnight. There were no cars or lights, no stealthy footsteps, no sounds at all but the plaintive calling of curlews across the marshes. In case her flashing headlights had failed to waken Charles she slammed the car door several times to announce her arrival. Then she lit the sitting-room lamp and stood silhouetted for a while in the doorway. The sky was partially overcast and the outline of Twinney Island was barely visible. The tide was right out.

She was just beginning to feel a little concerned at his lack of response when a sound reached her that no night bird could have made—a faint wolf whistle out of the darkness. Satisfied, she turned and began to consider the preparations she must make. He would want a good meal when he came and a hot drink and—since he would probably swim in naked to avoid getting his clothes wet— something to keep him warm while they talked. She fetched the rug from the car, and some wood for the sitting-room fire. As soon as she had got a cheerful blaze going she heated coffee and soup and filled two new vacuum flasks. Almost all the stores had disappeared from the larder, but she had foreseen that he might have visited the cottage in her absence and had brought plenty of food with her.

When she had done all she could in anticipation of his needs she turned the key in the lock and lay down on the settee to wait. The tides were much later than when she had been here last—it would be nearly four o'clock in the morning before there was enough water for him to get ashore without leaving marks. As the hours wore on she dozed fitfully, starting up in alarm when an ember fell into the grate or one of the old beams creaked. Her nerves were on edge. What she feared was a repetition of the sudden swoop that had brought on the first crisis.

But this time she wasn't disturbed, and at half-past three

she got up and went outside. The air had become very close, and she had a feeling that the long spell of fine weather might be drawing to an end. It looked as though she had come back none too soon.

By now the moon had risen behind the clouds and the line of the island was much clearer. The creek, already covered from bank to bank with gleaming water, looked tranquil and lovely; the soft gurgle of the flowing tide was soothing. Not much longer, she thought. In half an hour there would be a depth of two feet over the mud and that would be enough for him. She sat down on the shingle, listening and watching. Somewhere out there, across the ribbon of silver, he must be listening and watching too. Her excitement grew at the thought of his nearness. It seemed weeks since she had parted from him, and years since she had felt his arms around her.

Once she scrambled to her feet in haste as a light showed at the end of the causeway, but it was only the lamps of a night lorry on the main road and it soon passed. Once she went indoors to tend the fire. Slowly the minutes dragged by.

Then, at last, she heard a new sound from the direction of the island—the splash of water. He was coming! She opened the cottage door so that the light would guide him and gazed with straining eyes across the creek.

A shaft of moonlight suddenly broke through the clouds and in that moment she caught the gleam of his wet body and the white flash of his arms. He was swimming in fast. It seemed only a matter of seconds before he had struggled out on to the shingle and joined her.

"*Kathryn!*"

"Darling!" she said in a breathless whisper. "Oh, darling!" She drew him into the house and quickly shut the door.

He took her in his arms and held her close, his bearded face rough against her cheek. She felt the wetness of him soaking through her clothes but clung to him, oblivious of everything but the ecstasy of their meeting.

"Kathryn!" he murmured again, as though he couldn't say her name often enough. He twined her hair in his hands and pressed her head against his breast. "How I've longed for this!—just to have you back." He held her face so that he could look at her, and kissed her lips, and then drew her close to him again. "God, it's been lonely without you!"

"My love! You know I didn't want to leave you, don't you? I only went because it seemed the best way to get rid of the police. . . ."

"You've been wonderful, Kathryn, completely wonderful. I'm sure it was the right thing to do. . . ." He kissed her again, and released her with a sigh.

She became practical. "There's food all ready," she said. "We'll talk in a minute." She gave him the rug and made him sit by the fire while she fetched soup and ham and new brown bread.

He fell to ravenously. While he ate, she studied his face. "You've lost weight, darling. Do you feel all right?"

"I'm fine," he said. "Hard as nails."

"You look like the wild man of Borneo."

"I suppose I do. Well, it might be a useful disguise." He put the cup down and began to attack the pile of ham. "Has anything happened?—any new developments?"

"Not a thing. I've been staying quietly with John, and the hunt seems to have died right away. Now, Charles, tell me—*how* did you manage to hide that day? I was so certain they'd find you."

"They probably would have done if you hadn't worn that monstrosity of a dress, and given me time to prepare. They nearly did, as it was." Briefly, because it was an experience he wanted to forget, he told her how he'd buried himself in the mud. Kathryn listened with an expression of horror on her face.

"Darling—how *ghastly* for you."

"It wasn't exactly habit-forming."

"It must have been unspeakable. But it was a brilliant idea—I'd never have thought of it."

"Being hunted is very stimulating."

"Well, if anyone ever deserved to get away safely, you do. . . . What happened about the dinghy?"

He told her how he'd sunk the boat in the pool and hidden all the rest of the things in the mud. Presently he pushed his plate aside and sat back with a long sigh of satisfaction. "Gosh, that was good—I'd almost forgotten what real food tasted like. Sorry to make such a beast of myself!"

She lit a cigarette for him and poured out coffee. "How long will you be able to stay here?"

"Not more than an hour."

"Then we mustn't waste time. What are we going to do? Have you thought?"

"I've done nothing else but think." He drew slowly on his cigarette. "I believe there's only one hope for me. I'll have to take Peter's boat and somehow get myself across to France."

She looked at him aghast. "Do you think you can?"

"I can try."

"It sounds quite desperate—worse than anything yet."

"We *are* desperate. I won't pretend I like the idea, but what's the alternative?"

She wished she could have produced a cut-and-dried plan, but all she could say was, "Somehow or other to prove your innocence, I suppose."

He shook his head. "It's not realistic, darling. There are only two possible ways of doing that—to find out who really killed Louise or to establish my alibi for the time when she was killed—and I don't see any prospect of doing either."

"I'm not so sure," she said earnestly. "I did some thinking, too, while I was at Norwich—about Louise, and those hotel visits of hers. I'm certain we were right about her meeting some man—she just wasn't the sort of woman to go away on her own. And if we could discover who it was . . ."

"But all that was gone into at the time."

"Oh, I know Fairey employed inquiry agents, but we don't really know how good they were, do we? They may have been most efficient, but I always felt I'd much sooner trust myself on a job like that, and I still do. I believe if I went to stay at those hotels I might find out something."

He considered. "You might, but I frankly doubt it. I agree it's well worth trying—but not at this moment. Even if you did make some discovery, it would take ages to prove anything. What would I be doing in the meantime?"

"Couldn't I hide you in the flat now that the police are leaving me alone?"

"They won't go on leaving you alone if I don't show up

pretty soon—especially if you suddenly start making hotel inquiries. It'll merely confirm their suspicions that we're in touch."

"Well, couldn't you stay on the island just a little longer? Oh, darling, I know it's horrible for you, it must seem as though you're the only person left alive in the world, but at least it's safe. We could easily stock it with provisions now that we're not being watched, and we might even fix up some sort of shelter for you. It would give me a chance—even if I only had a week or two."

"I daren't risk it. I can take the discomfort—that isn't what worries me. The thing is, if I *am* going to get to the Continent I must do it at once, before the weather breaks. If I miss my chance now I may find myself stuck here, and I don't believe anyone could survive a winter on Twinney Island."

She gave an involuntary shiver. "That's impossible, of course—but surely there's *some* place you could hide—somewhere a bit more comfortable, where I could still keep you supplied?"

"Let's face it, Kathryn—there isn't. Not in England. I'm too well known by now and everybody's on the lookout for me. We've survived these few days because we've had a lot of luck and the weather's been perfect, but if we try our luck too far we shall come to grief. Something will go wrong—one of us will make a mistake, and that will be the end. If I stay in this country I shall be caught—there's nothing as certain as that. It's a hard thing to have to admit, but flight is my only chance—and the sooner the better."

Kathryn studied his drawn, determined face and suddenly she knew that any more argument would be a waste of breath. "You've made up your mind, haven't you?"

"Yes, my love. I think I must take the boat while I can."

"All right," she said quietly. "When do we start?"

"I'll have to make the crossing alone."

"You know I won't let you do that."

"I must, Kathryn. I'm not just trying to save you a bad trip—I've worked it all out and there's no other way. I don't mean that you shouldn't come to France, but you've got to be there strictly on the level, with a properly stamped passport. Then you, at least, will be able to move about and make arrangements without fear of the police. You'll be able to change money at the banks, for one thing—they always want to see one's passport. You'll be able to travel freely, too—you'll be able to come back to England any time you like and see lawyers and people. You'll be able to make those hotel inquiries later on. But if we both go over in *Witch* and land surreptitiously we'll neither of us have any freedom—we'll both be hamstrung."

"Yes, I see that, of course," she said slowly.

"What I suggest is that you go back to town and collect your foreign currency allowance and your passport and a case of things, and then cross openly to Calais and wait for me there. I can't be sure when I'll arrive, but whenever it is I'll try to make a landfall after dark and we must have elastic arrangements about meeting. After that, we'll decide on the next step."

"Will you still have to keep hidden?"

"I expect so, up to a point, but it'll be much safer there than here. Of course, the French police may have been warned to keep an eye open for me, but they're more casual than our own police and at least my face won't be known to every man and woman in the street. And there's the climate to think of—we can work our way down south and even if I have to sleep out for a while it won't matter. . . ." He caught her look of dismay. "I'm sorry, sweetheart, I'm afraid it's not much of a prospect and I'll still have to rely on you at every turn. . . ."

"That's not what's worrying me," she said. "It's the practical difficulties. For one thing, a single travel allowance isn't going to last us long. What shall we do for francs when it's gone?"

"There must be ways of getting hold of more—other people seem to manage it. I don't think that'll be an insuperable problem."

"Perhaps not." Kathryn thought of the friends in Paris who might help her. "But how is it going to end? We can't go on living from hand to mouth in a strange country for ever. Of course, if I have any luck at the hotels it will be different, but suppose my inquiries don't come to anything . . .?"

"It's no good looking too far into the future at this stage. First let's get out of England."

136

She met his gaze unhappily, thinking again of the long voyage in *Witch*. Suddenly she said: "Charles, surely when the police hear that a Medway boat has been abandoned off the French coast they're bound to guess that it was you who took her? And then they'll know where you've landed."

"I thought of that," he said. "I'm afraid I'll have to sink her off shore. I shall hate doing it, but we can get Peter a new boat in the end, and I'm sure he'll forgive me."

She nodded—it was a measure of their desperation that the scuttling of a friend's boat seemed almost a trifling matter. For a while she sat in dejected silence, thinking about the plan.

"Well, I suppose it might work," she said at last, "and I do realise how important it is that I should be free to move about. All the same, I can't bear to think of you attempting that trip by yourself. How far is it to Calais?"

"About eighty or ninety miles from here if I keep fairly close to the coast."

"That means that even if everything goes well you'll have to be at sea for at least two nights, doesn't it? And *Witch* is such a tiny boat."

"She's a good sea-boat—I always feel much more comfortable in her than in *Spray*. I shall manage. After all, plenty of other men have crossed to France by themselves in small boats."

"Other men are used to the sea—you're not. I know we've pottered about in the estuary quite a bit but you can't pretend you're really experienced and you've done hardly any sailing by yourself. If the weather turns bad you'll get exhausted. Don't you remember how utterly worn out we were that day we crossed from Harty Ferry to Brightlingsea, even with two of us to share the chores?—and that was an easy passage."

"I know, darling. Still, it's no use dwelling on that when there's no alternative."

"Couldn't I come part of the way with you?"

"*Part* of the way? How?"

"Well, we'd have to work it all out, of course, but you'll have a dinghy and I should think you could put me ashore near Dover after dark if we timed it carefully. I'd be with you for three-quarters of the trip then, and you'd only have the actual channel crossing to do by yourself. That wouldn't be so bad."

"It would be taking a hell of a chance. Timing things carefully in a small boat isn't very easy."

"Darling, it's easy if the weather's good, you know that, and if the weather turns foul that's just when you're going to need me. If the worst came to the worst we'd just *have* to go on together. After all, what's the point of my getting to France with a nice legal passport if you've drowned yourself on the way?" She was as determined now as he was. "Honestly, I think it's absolutely crazy for you to try that trip single-handed."

"It's crazy to try it at all, but there's no other way."

"At least there's a little more hope if we both go. I admit I'm not much good with boats but I can hold the tiller while you get some rest and that's the most important thing. Charles, you know I'm right about this. Take me to Dover."

For a while, he didn't answer her. It wasn't an easy decision. There was the personal risk to Kathryn, and the chance that he might not be able to land her. But he knew in his heart that she was right about the single-handed passage. The least bit of bad weather would defeat him.

"All right, darling," he said at last. "We'll start together, anyhow."

She smiled. "That's better. Now we can really get down to things."

Part Three

CHAPTER I

CHARLES sat on top of the island sea-wall and looked out over the empty creek for the last time. Nearly twenty-four hours had elapsed since he and Kathryn had agreed on their respective tasks, and the hands of the rusty old alarm clock that he'd brought over from the cottage in a waterproof toilet bag pointed to two. Four hours to dawn—and a strenuous night's work to get through! On the whole, conditions favoured his enterprise. The sky was cloudy again, but there would be enough moonlight for him to see what he was doing.

He felt excited and more than a little apprehensive at the thought of what lay ahead. His life had not been a particularly sheltered one, but nothing in it had prepared him for the kind of heroic physical adventure to which he was now committed. Camping out in the bush seemed a very tame affair by comparison—and then he had had plenty of helpers. Even on those rare occasions when there had been labour troubles in the cane-fields and he had got mixed up in ugly situations, there had always been resolute men to handle them. Now he had not merely to take decisions but to execute them personally with his own two hands. Wryly he recalled Louise's taunt—"Such an active man—but hardly a man of action!" It had been true enough when she'd said it, he thought, but it was scarcely true now. The species had changed in order to survive.

At a quarter past two he drew on his sea-boots, scrambled down the wall, and set off across the mud to recover the dinghy. There was a firm bottom near the shore and at first he hardly sank above his ankles, but as he got farther away from the island he came across soft, knee-deep patches where it was all he could do to take another step. In the lonely darkness, the journey was eerie and frightening. Once he lost his balance altogether and fell sprawling in the muck; once a foot came up without its boot and he had to pull and heave on the slippery rubber with his hands before the mud yielded it up with a reluctant plop. Behind him he left a deep, ineradicable trail which he knew would outlast many tides. But that no longer worried him—with luck, he would be out of reach before anyone became interested.

As he advanced, the going became heavier, the scene more desolate. He was ploughing through a squelchy sepia waste, with no water or land visible and no distinguishing features to guide him. A luminous patch of cloud over the moon gave him a rough idea of his direction, but he had been forced to make several detours and soon he had only the vaguest idea where he was. He would have liked to stop and consider, but the pull of the mud warned him that he might get stuck unless he kept moving. When at last he caught a distant gleam from the pool where he had concealed the dinghy, he thought he had never seen a more welcome sight.

Locating the boat took longer than he had expected. He had sunk it at high water after sounding with a line improvised from the tarred twine he had picked up under the island wall. At low tide, if his calculations had been right, it should have been lying at the edge of the pool, easily accessible, but at first he could see no sign of it. Then his probing foot stubbed on the dinghy's painter where it joined the tiny anchor buried in the mud bank, and by following the rope he found the boat in nearly three feet of water. The incoming tide was just beginning to flow—he had cut things dangerously fine. He stripped off his clothes, rolled them into a bundle, and put them up on the bank. Then, from under the thwarts, he began to lug out the heavy stones that he'd used to weight the dinghy. He had to work half-submerged, with the mud dragging at his legs and the thick water running into his eyes.

Even when his groping fingers told him that all the stones were out, it wasn't easy to haul the boat from the pool. The mud was getting softer as the rising water seeped through it, and by now the whole bank was churned into a morass in which he staggered and floundered like a drunken man. Sweat poured off him as he tugged and heaved. Little by little the stern came up and out until he was able to bale and lighten the load. At last, with the tide swirling round his feet, he managed to tip the dinghy on to its side, drain it, and refloat it. He unfastened the oars which were tied across the thwarts and snapped the strings that secured the rowlocks. "Tender to *Spray*" was in commission again.

He got his damp clothes and thankfully climbed aboard. It had been a hard struggle but he had done it, and he felt a glow of achievement. There was no hurry now. The warm, close air soon dried him and he dressed again. For a while he was content to let the dinghy drift with the young flood, knowing that the stream was setting him towards the cottage, which was his next stopping place. By the time the gaunt outline of the roof appeared against the sky the water was deep enough for him to row, and he pulled quietly in to the shingle and made fast.

Before leaving for London that morning Kathryn had made a quick trip into Rochester and laid in essential stores —a four-gallon jerrycan of petrol, a tin of oil, paraffin for the lamps and stove, a bottle of methylated spirit, and a quantity of fresh and canned food. For safety, she had hidden them away in the long matted grass of the saltings some twenty yards from the cottage, watched by Charles from the island. Now he proceeded to clear the dump and load the things into the dinghy. When everything was transferred he gathered up a few oddments that Kathryn had left ready in the sitting-room, locked the cottage, and sculled the boat across to *Spray*. From the tiny cabin he took charts and tide tables, and from under the floorboards a dozen lumps of pig-iron ballast which he would need later on. Then he rowed back to the island to pick up the rest of the gear—a can of fresh water, his own sleeping-bag, the tarpaulin, and the precious binoculars. When he had finished, the dinghy was stacked to the gunwales. He cast a last unsentimental glance around the place that had been his home for a week and pushed the boat off from the "hard".

By now the creek was almost full and the surface of the water was as smooth and motionless as quicksilver. The next stage of the journey should be less arduous, for he would have the ebb with him. Balancing carefully on the seat to avoid any possibility of an upset he began to row with long, steady strokes, heading out for the buoys that marked the main channel of the Medway. If he and Kathryn were to take full advantage of the hours of darkness on the following night, it was essential that tonight he should establish himself at an advanced base where deep water would be accessible to the dinghy at all states of the tide.

As he slid past the chain of strung-out islands, his main concern was to keep the heavily-laden boat well clear of the shallows. He had made this trip several times before, but never at night, and in the darkness it would be fatally easy to get caught on one of the extensive banks and find himself high and dry as the tide went down. Repeatedly he glanced over his shoulder, checking his approximate course by a distant flashing buoy. Once or twice he stopped and took soundings with an oar.

He had been rowing for almost an hour when the loom of a triangular beacon, rising from the hump of a small island, told him he had reached his destination. It was a place he knew well, for Kathryn and he had often picnicked here in the old days. There was a narrow inlet that snaked between mud walls and after a little manœuvring he got the dinghy in and ran it aground. Over the hump was the busy deep channel, but on this side of the island he would be quite secluded.

He had finished his journey just in time—already there was a glow of morning in the east and a luminous sheen on the water. He sat resting beside the boat, listening to the throb of a ship's engine and wondering what the next dawn would bring.

The day slipped quickly by, for he had plenty to occupy his mind. Most of the long passage that lay ahead would be through waters that were unfamiliar to him, and the more he could learn about the shoals and buoys beforehand, the better chance he and Kathryn would have if conditions became tough. The handsome yachting chart, with its blue-and-brown sea contours and its boldly-indicated shipping lanes, made a voyage round the coast of Kent look as simple as a drive up the Great North Road, but Charles was not deceived. With anxious care he studied the route which he hoped would bring them to Dover at sundown on the second night. He memorised the position of buoys with curious-sounding names—the Grain Hard and the Spile, the Horse and the Longnose—and the light signals they would give out after dark. He examined the coastal outlines in the illustrated *North Sea Pilot*, wondering if he would be able to identify any of them from the sea. He even spent some time poring over a complicated diagram that showed the speed and set of the tides. When he felt satisfied that he could do no more without hopelessly confusing himself, he spread out his kapok bag and turned in. He had heavy arrears of sleep to make up, and he would need to be fresh for the night's start.

No one came near the island all day. He dozed most of the morning, and in the afternoon he took all the gear out of the dinghy and carefully restowed it so that it would be less in his way during the long row to Upnor. When the tide came in he floated the boat out to the edge of the saltings and anchored it there, ready for the launching later. A light westerly wind had brought more cloud and he didn't much like the way the weather was shaping, but at least the wind was fair and would give them a good slant out of the river without any need for the engine.

Long before dusk he was impatient to get away. He watched the saltings uncover and the fringe of mud re-emerge around the island and the light slowly fade from the sky. As soon as it seemed safe to make a move he seized the loaded dinghy by the bows and dragged it down the smooth wet slipway to the water. The ebb was well advanced and the tide was racing down against him. It was going to be a hard row. He settled himself squarely in the centre of the boat, jammed his feet against the petrol can for leverage, and pulled out into the main channel.

For a while he hugged the southern shore, keeping so close to the margin that occasionally his starboard oar touched the bottom. His knowledge of the local currents was limited, but he knew that tidal streams usually ran less fiercely near the bank. Out in the middle of the river he could see the moving lights of ships, but here he was all on his own and could concentrate on his rowing without worrying about other traffic. He pulled with short, stabbing strokes as he had seen experts do against the tide, grunting a little with the exertion. Once more, sweat began to roll off him.

Presently he came to the mouth of a wide tributary creek —Half Acre Creek, he noted, with satisfaction at his progress. He made for a red-flashing buoy on the other side and crept slowly along the edge of a sheet of mud called Bishop Ooze, where he and Kathryn had once run aground in *Spray* on the top of a falling tide. They had joked, he remembered, about the name of the Reach—Long Reach —because they had been marooned there for nearly twelve hours. Happy days, when the worst that could happen was a minor misadventure!

An hour's steady rowing brought him to a point where the river narrowed and took a sharp bend to the left. To reach Upnor, he would have to cross to the northern bank, and this seemed as good a place as any. Resting for a moment on his oars, he listened carefully to make sure that no ships were approaching. They could appear so quickly, and from a high bridge he would be quite invisible. But the channel seemed quiet, and he turned the dinghy's head and pulled with all his strength for the opposite shore. The ebb carried him down a little, but in a few minutes he was over the fairway and could breathe freely again. As he swung upstream once more, he calculated that he was more than half-way to *Witch*.

It was very dark now—much darker than it had been on the previous night. He could only guess the time, but already he felt as though he had been rowing for hours. His hands were stiff and blistered and his shoulders ached abominably. His only consolation was that the adverse tide was beginning to slacken—he no longer had the feeling that every stroke was a battle. Once he had cleared the beacon off Folly Point the improvement became even more noticeable and he settled down in good heart for the long pull past the Hoo flats. On the other side of the river, not so very far ahead, the lights of Chatham and Gillingham blazed cheerfully. Opposite them was Upnor.

He sought refuge from tiredness in a child's game, counting his strokes and resolutely refusing to turn and note his progress until a hundred had gone by. When that palled, he switched his thoughts to Kathryn, wondering if she had managed to get through her heavy schedule and whether she would be waiting for him on the bank. He thought of *Witch* and mentally rehearsed the jobs he would have to do when he reached her. Slowly the distance lessened. Soon there were lights on his side of the river, too—this time from warships moored off the fairway in the Hoo bend. There seemed to be a good deal of activity aboard, and he gave them a wide berth. Little by little he closed the Upnor shore, working his way in until he could see the outline of the thickly-wooded hill behind the anchorage. A final spurt brought him into shallow water and suddenly his oars grated on stones. Then, at last, he rested.

No sound came from the beach—it looked as though he had beaten Kathryn to the rendezvous. He still had to find *Witch*, though, and as he gazed around he realised that the turquoise hull wouldn't be easy to pick out in the darkness. Peter had always kept his boat well to the east of the congested Upnor moorings, but now other people seemed to have had the same idea and the congestion had spread. On all sides, dark shapes loomed up out of the water like the hulls of a blacked-out convoy, and identification would be possible only at close range. With a new sense of urgency he seized the oars and began to row from boat to boat.

For twenty minutes he combed the eastern anchorage. At first he felt no uneasiness—he knew more or less where to look and it could only be a matter of time before he found her. But as he continued to search without success, anxiety grew. There was no doubt about it—*Witch* wasn't where she should have been. Either Peter had changed her moorings or—ghastly thought!—he had chartered her to someone and she wasn't at Upnor at all!

Thoroughly alarmed now, he extended his search to the western end. One thing was certain—they'd have to take somebody's boat. *Spray* was much too small to make a long passage, and in any case there was no way of getting back to her tonight. Their plans were too far advanced to be changed.

His mind was just beginning to grapple with new and intractable problems when, glancing over his shoulder as he pulled away from a small racing yacht, he saw the outline of a hull that seemed familiar. A moment later his eager fingers were exploring the bows, fumbling for the embossed letters that should be there. Yes, there were letters . . .! He spelt them out—W-I-T-C-H. He mopped his face with his wet sleeve, breathing hard. She *had* been moved.

But as his agitation died down he saw that she was well-placed at the outer edge of the anchorage. She'd be easy to take away.

Now that he had found *Witch* he began to feel concerned about Kathryn. Either she was very late in arriving or, more probably, she had slipped past him in the darkness and was waiting at the other end of the moorings where they'd arranged to meet. She might realise what had happened, of course, but if she didn't show up soon he'd have to go and look for her. Meanwhile, he'd do better to get on with the chores. He made the dinghy fast, removed the cockpit cover, and climbed aboard. The key was in its place on a hook inside one of the lockers and he opened up the cabin.

Witch was a Bermuda-rigged sloop—twenty feet long on the waterline, with a draught of four feet and a beam of seven-foot-six. She had been built for safe and comfortable cruising rather than for speed, and though her canoe-shaped stern cut down space in the cockpit she had a roomy cabin, conventionally laid out with a table between two bunks and a galley just inside the starboard bulkhead. Her generous lines gave her plenty of stability, and Peter had always spoken with pride of her steadiness in a seaway. Charles sincerely hoped he was right.

He set to work at once to transfer the gear from the dinghy. There was a lot of stuff and it had to be stowed methodically, some of it in the forepeak and cabin and some in the lockers. When that job was finished he removed the sail cover, sorted out the sheets and halyards, and made sure there was petrol in the tank in case they should need the engine at short notice. In addition to the four gallons he had brought with him he found another full jerrycan aboard, which meant they would have fuel for twenty hours' steaming if the need should arise.

The problem of navigation lights worried him. There were *pros* and *cons*, but on the whole it seemed wiser to carry them. In favour was the fact that the mouth of the Medway was narrow and busy and that an unlit boat might easily be run down in the darkness. Police and harbour launches were often active there, too, and if *Witch* did happen to be spotted without lights there would certainly be questions. Against was the fact that the departure of a lighted yacht from the estuary might be observed and recorded in some official log. But it was a common enough occurrence, particularly at this time of year, and nobody was likely to give it a second thought. Besides, *Witch's* absence from her moorings was bound to be noticed—the hope was that people would think Peter had returned and taken her away himself. In the end Charles decided to light the lamps as soon as the boat was under way.

At that moment, over towards the trees, he heard the crunch of feet on pebbles. He waited tensely, not certain that it was Kathryn. Then a low whistle set his fears at rest. He whistled back, and thankfully untied the dinghy. Half a dozen strokes took him to the shore. The footfalls came nearer, and Kathryn emerged out of the darkness.

"Thank heavens!" she said in a tremulous whisper. "I've been searching for you everywhere."

"Sorry, darling—the boat's been moved. I scarcely knew what to do."

"Is everything all right?"

"Yes, we're almost ready to go. Let's look for Peter's dinghy."

"Shall we need it?"

"I daren't leave it behind. Someone would be sure to think it odd."

After a brief search they found the boat drawn out at the top of the bank and dragged it quickly to the water's edge. Kathryn climbed in and Charles towed it across to *Witch* and secured it. Then he proceeded to dispose of his own dinghy. Making sure that he had left nothing in it except the iron ballast, he pushed its bows down under the water. It began to fill, became waterlogged, gave a protesting gurgle, and sank slowly in three fathoms.

"All right," he said softly. "Let's go."

The tide was slack and the boat was lying head to wind, so that getting away presented no problem. Charles hoisted the tall sail and made the halyard fast. Kathryn stood by the tiller. There was a gentle splash as the mooring buoy went overboard, and with the foresail backed *Witch's* head began to pay off to port. The boom swung over with a rattle of blocks, the mainsail filled, and Kathryn took the slight strain. A faint chuckle of water rose from the stern and the shoreline slowly receded.

They were off!

For a few minutes Charles busied himself on the cabin top, lighting the lamps and coiling down the ropes. Then he joined Kathryn in the cockpit. "Well, we've managed it!" he said with satisfaction. "Did you have a very frightful day?"

"It was a bit rushed, but everything went off all right. The bank said it was short notice for the money, but they got it for me."

"Passport okay?"

"Yes." She gave her pocket a slap. "And the suitcase is in the cloakroom at Dover."

"What about the car?"

"I left it in town and came down by train—it's what I'd have done if I'd really been going on an innocent trip."

He nodded, easing the sheet a little. "Did anyone think it odd when you bought all those stores yesterday?"

"No, I got them at several different shops."

"Anyone recognise you?"

"I don't think so. I made myself up quite differently— I don't think even you would have known me."

"Then with luck we should have a long start. What's the time, darling?"

She peered. "Nearly half past eleven."

"Aren't you tired?"

"No, only excited."

He smiled. "We'll have to keep proper watches when we get out of the river."

She asked him about his journey upstream and he told her. After that they sat silently hand in hand, watching the lovely curve of the sail and listening to the hiss of the wake. The river was calm, the red and green reflections of the navigation lamps on the water were cosy and reassuring, the effortless glide of the ship was soothing. Although they were off on a desperate adventure, a sense of peace gradually stole over them as the anchorage fell away astern. Of peace, and of hope. Ahead was the familiar well-lit channel, the beckoning flash of buoys—and the sea.

The wind was light but steady and they were soon making good progress over the tide. By keeping just outside the line of buoys they could be sure of sufficient depth to clear their keel without getting in the way of heavier traffic. Presently Charles passed the tiller to Kathryn and went below to light the cabin lamp and make sure that everything was ship-shape and well-stowed. As far as he could see, *Witch* had all the gear aboard that they were likely to need, and some that he would hardly know how to use. There was a spare bower anchor and kedge and a stout warp in the fore-peak; storm sails in a locker; two sets of oilskins on a peg; life-jackets in a rack; and a sea-anchor. Among Peter's charts he found one of the English channel, which would come in useful for the second leg of the passage.

His spirits were high now that they were under way, but he had a nasty shock when he tapped the barometer on the cabin bulkhead. The needle took a sharp plunge downwards. His face became rather solemn, but he decided to keep the bad news to himself.

Kathryn was concentrating on the steering when he emerged, and she looked very much the yachtswoman. By the light of the cabin lamp he could see now that she was wearing slacks and a jersey, with a windcheater over the top. Her thick hair was stuffed into a beret. She smiled happily as he came up on deck.

"All in order?" she asked.

"Apple-pie." He stooped and flashed a torch into the bilge. "H'm!—I think I'll pump her out. We may as well start dry, anyway."

By the time the pump began to suck air they were rounding Folly Point, and he took over again as the wind came abeam. "What about a spot of food now," he suggested, "while everything's nice and quiet?"

"Tea and sandwiches?"

"Fine . . .! Oh, and I should make a few extra while you're about it," he added casually.

She read nothing sinister into the instruction and went below to get the stove going. Charles noted the number of a buoy as it slipped past their quarter and checked their exact position on the chart. They were certainly covering the ground—provided the wind held steady they should be out of the estuary well before daybreak. If only the weather had been a bit more promising! The thought of the falling glass nagged at him continually. *Witch* was a sound boat, of course—twenty feet of good oak and workmanship. With enough competent hands she'd be safe in any sea—after all, five-tonners had crossed the Atlantic more than once.   But that was the difficulty—there weren't enough competent hands, and in a storm the boat would easily outsail the crew.

For a moment he watched Kathryn's absorbed face as she sat on one of the berths buttering bread and opening tins, and he thought how wonderfully matter-of-fact she was, how content to trust him now that they were embarked on the trip.   It made his responsibility all the greater.   With a troubled frown, he turned again to the chart.

The food tasted excellent, and the cigarette that followed even better.   The feeling that they no longer had to rush was very pleasant.   By the time the meal was over Charles reckoned that they must be passing the island where he had spent the day.   The river was wider now, and surprisingly empty.   In a whole hour they had seen nothing but a tug and one small steamer, going upstream on the tide.   Except for the buoys, there were no lights anywhere.   When they talked, it was in subdued voices, for there was something awe-inspiring about the spacious darkness.

As the flood strengthened against the wind the motion of the boat became livelier and "Tender to *Witch*" began to yaw about at the end of its towline.   Charles watched it uneasily for a while.   The dinghy was vital to them—if anything happened to it they would be crippled.   He wished they could have put it on the cabin roof, but there simply wasn't room.   In the end he did the next best thing and substituted two new lengths of manila line for the single painter.

After that there were no more anxieties until they approached the congested exit from the estuary.   Then they both became very alert.   On either side of the fairway, vessels were moored—destroyers, old mine-sweepers, dredgers, barges, and occasionally a big cargo ship.   The tide was sluicing in fast, and they had a worrying moment or two when a stationary ship took their wind and the sails started to flap.   Short steep seas were beginning to fling them about so that they had to hang on to the sides of the cockpit for support.   Steering was becoming more difficult, and once they missed a huge unlighted buoy by inches. Charles had always thought this a hateful spot, even in the daytime.

But they were getting very near the mouth now.   On the

port bow he could see the white flash of the Grain Hard buoy; ahead, the red beacon on Garrison Point. Suddenly he saw something else—the red, white and green that could only mean a vessel approaching head on. A moment later the quietness of the night was shattered by a single short blast on the ship's siren.

"An empty river, and then we meet something *here*!" Charles muttered between his teeth. He turned *Witch* to starboard a little, struggling with the kicking tiller as vicious little waves pounded at the rudder. There was still way on the yacht, but not very much, and he feared he might lose control of her altogether. Two lights on the land crept by each other at a snail's pace. Perhaps he ought to start the engine! Perhaps he was still in the fairway!

Then the green light of the steamer slowly dimmed, and the red grew brighter. They were all right! Now they were slipping past the stone breakwater of Garrison Point. They heard the thud of powerful engines and in a moment a huge ship loomed out of the darkness, hung over them, and passed less than a cable away. The bow wave caught them and tossed them about like dice in a box. A brief respite, and the stern wave followed, not quite so bad. Then *Witch* became manageable again. The river widened; on their starboard quarter Garrison Point slowly receded. Charles switched on the binnacle lamp and set the yacht on her compass course. Ahead of them lay the open sea.

CHAPTER II

THE tossing they had gone through in the river mouth had given Kathryn a headache, and when Charles suggested that she should go below for a while she made no protest. He watched her wriggle into one of the bags and draw the rug up around her and presently he knew she was asleep. He would give her a couple of hours, he decided, and at day-break—if she felt up to it—he would get her to take over.

Now that they were out of the estuary he was able to relax a little. It was true that he could see a lot more lights than the chart had led him to expect, but as long as he stuck to his course and didn't actually run into anything he should be all right. Visibility was good, and now that he had room to manœuvre he felt less nervous about other shipping. The warm breeze that fanned the back of his neck was keeping the sails nicely filled, and as *Witch* drew away from the land and the tide slackened, the viciousness began to go out of the waves. Soon the boat had settled to a steady rhythm, a buoyant rise and fall that was by no means unpleasant. The dinghy, which had behaved alarmingly in the estuary mouth, was again riding quietly in the smooth wake.

Conditions were so peaceful, indeed, that Charles was lulled by the motion and found it increasingly difficult to concentrate on the compass. The long row to Upnor had tired him even more than he had realised, and his body craved sleep. Such sounds as there were only made him drowsier—the light tapping of the halyards against the mast, the creaking of a block as he eased the mainsheet, the gentle susurrous of the sea as it slipped away under the stern But. every time his head gave a nod the boat went off course and the swinging boom roused him again. Some yachts, he had heard, could sail themselves, but *Witch* evidently wasn't one of them.

Just before six o'clock, by the light of a sullen dawn, he made out a black shape on the port bow and steered towards it. As he had hoped, it turned out to be the Spile buoy. He felt encouraged—so far, the calculations he had made on the island had worked out well. He called softly to Kathryn and she woke at once and came into the cockpit.

"Feeling better?" he asked her.

"I'm a new woman," she told him, with a bright morning smile. She sat down beside him, slipping her arm through his and momentarily scanning his face. Then she looked round at the lowering sky and the heaving waste of water and her smile faded. "How are we doing?"

"Not too badly. I think that must be Warden Point over there."

She followed the direction of his finger and gave an involuntary shiver. The land was no more than a shadowy outline and it seemed a very long way away. Though she had never admitted it to Charles, she had always been scared of the open sea. Sailing about in the shallow, sheltered creeks of the Medway had been pleasant enough, but on the rare occasions when they had ventured outside the river she had always felt secretly relieved when they had made port safely, even though they had been in no danger. It was a purely physical reaction in the face of a potentially terrifying element—her nerves were always well under control but her mind shrank at the thought of the depth and the vastness. Some people, she knew, saw the sea as a surface, a two-dimensional plane on which boats floated. She always saw it as three-dimensional, as something that could overwhelm and swallow her. She had an idea that Charles thought about it in the same way. Probably they would never have had anything to do with boats at all if they hadn't been practically forced into it by circumstances.

"At least the water's a lot smoother now," she said.

"Yes, there's not so much wind. If it drops any more I suppose we'll have to use the engine, but I think we're all right for the moment—the tide should be taking us the way we want to go. Do you feel like steering for a bit?"

"Of course, darling—you must be dead."

"Not yet!" he said grimly. He gave her the tiller. "If you keep the compass needle around 110 you won't go far wrong."

"When shall I call you?"

"Eight o'clock—not later. Give me a shout if there's any trouble."

She nodded, and he stumbled below.

He was wakened just before eight by the incongruous sound of a B.B.C. announcer's voice from the cockpit—Kathryn was listening to the shipping forecast on the portable radio. From what he could hear of it the outlook had deteriorated, and when he sat up and tapped the barometer his impression was confirmed. He scrambled out of his bag and went on deck.

The sky certainly looked much more menacing. It was almost as dark now as it had been at six, and away to the north there were rumblings that sounded like thunder. The wind had dropped to the lightest of light airs and *Witch* was ghosting over a calm and oily sea. There were one or two steamers hull down on the horizon, but Charles could see no sign of any sea marks.

"Any idea where we are?" he asked, glancing at the compass.

"Not really," Kathryn confessed. "I did see a buoy about an hour ago but it wasn't near enough for me to read the name."

He studied the chart for a few moments but failed to come to any definite conclusion. The shore was even farther away now, flat and featureless. He had a notion that they must be off the mouth of the Swale, but if so they had made very poor progress lately.

"I think we'd better start the engine," he said.

Kathryn agreed a little apprehensively. The four horse-power motor was the same kind as the one they had in *Spray* and she knew how temperamental it could be. Once it was going properly it would run like a clock all day, but it often gave starting trouble when it had been left untended for some time.

Today proved to be no exception. It sprang into life at the second swing but after it had run for a few minutes it gave a cough and died away with a depressing rattle of the starting chain. Charles thought he knew what the trouble was—there must be an air lock in the pipe. He tried blowing through the filler cap of the petrol tank but the lock didn't clear and reluctantly he got out the tools. Peter had taught him rule-of-thumb methods for dealing with this and other simple problems, but he had no real feeling for engines and he knew he was as likely to strip a thread or lose an important nut in the bilge as to cure the trouble. The knowledge that today he couldn't afford to make a mistake made him more nervous than usual and it took him a long while to unscrew and reassemble the pipe. By the time he had finished, the cockpit reeked of petrol and he was filthy in appearance and temper. He flooded the carburettor and flung himself on the handle, turning until he was exhausted. The thing remained obdurately dead. At last he sat back on his heels, nursing his blisters, while Kathryn regarded him anxiously. In a situation like this she felt quite helpless, and she knew that silence was better than suggestion. They had been through it all before.

He continued to gaze at the engine as though it were a malevolent monster, trying to remember what Peter had told him to do. By now *Witch* had lost almost all her way and was slowly drifting on the tide with drooping sails. They were wasting valuable time, and if he couldn't get the damn' thing going they might be here for hours. Perhaps he'd overflooded her. He took the plug out and cleaned it and turned the handle a few times to clear the cylinder, and when he put it back the motor started at once and ran sweetly. He gave Kathryn a rather sheepish smile and thankfully put the tools away, licking the blood from a couple of damaged knuckles. Though the engine was noisy and made conversation difficult in the cockpit, the sound was like music in their ears. *Witch* had a fine white wake again, and at a steady five knots they would cover a lot of ground. He washed the oil from his hands and took the tiller while Kathryn went below to prepare breakfast. It was their first proper meal for a long time and she made it a good one—bacon and eggs and marmalade, and coffee brewed in a jug.

The hot food heartened her, but Charles became more and more silent as the meal progressed and presently she could stand it no longer.

"What's wrong, darling?" she asked.

"Only the weather! It's lunacy to stay out here in a small boat with the glass dropping like a stone."

She gazed round at the quiet pewter-coloured water, the heavy, almost motionless banks of cloud. "It doesn't look too bad."

"This is the calm before the storm—the barometer doesn't lie. I'm wondering if we oughtn't to try to reach the Swale—it can't be more than three or four miles away. In an hour we could be in sheltered waters again."

"And then what?"

"Wait till the storm's over, I suppose."

"Charles, you know we can't afford to do that—we might be stuck there for days. They're bound to find out before long that *Witch* has been taken, and if anyone noticed her in the Swale you'd be caught. We've *got* to go on."

"All hell may break loose soon."

"It can't be worse than the hell we've been through already."

"You may be drowned. I'm risking your life, and I don't think I've the right to."

"We went over all that before."

"We didn't know then that the weather was going to let us down. Now we do."

"It may not be as bad as you think. Besides, aren't there any other places where we could shelter if we had to—farther along?"

"It may be too late then."

"I'd sooner take a chance. Come on, drink your coffee and stop worrying."

He said no more, but she saw that he was still very troubled. Presently he climbed up on to the cabin top and tucked a precautionary reef in the mainsail. In a flat calm that was a simple matter, even for him. Later, it might be impossible.

As the morning wore on, he began to believe that they might be lucky after all. Though the roll of distant thunder was now incessant and the peaked, purple clouds were shot with lightning flashes, the storm seemed unable to break. The engine was still running perfectly, and with the help of the tide they must be doing seven or eight miles an hour over the ground. In the gunmetal light it was becoming harder to identify the buoys but just before eleven he made out the black and white chequers of the

Horse, which marked the entrance to the deep water channel called the Gore. As the tide slackened, their pace slowed, but by noon they were abreast of Margate and still going well. Kathryn, coming up from a spell below, was astonished at the progress they'd made.

"How far to Dover now?" she asked.

Charles considered. "About forty miles I suppose."

"And how far have we come?"

"About thirty."

"Why, we're doing fine, darling."

He grunted.

At that moment the rain started. There were a few warning plops on the deck, splashes the size of half-crowns, and suddenly the sky cracked open. Kathryn dived for Charles's oilskins and thrust them at him. Then she crouched inside the cabin, watching the water sheeting past the door. The sight was impressive; the noise as it struck the cabin top was so great that she could barely hear the engine any more. Outside, an opaque curtain had closed down over the sea, cutting visibility to feet. The sails hung like sodden rags. Charles cowered by the tiller, taking the full force of the vertical shafts of rain and steering by the compass when he could see it. Water filled his ears and eyes, sluiced off his sou'wester, trickled down his neck, poured into his sea-boots. The bilge rose so quickly that he feared it might reach the engine and called Kathryn out to pump. He'd often seen such rain in the Caribbean, but rarely here at home. Still, it wasn't affecting the boat's progress—so far, things might have been a lot worse.

For more than half an hour the deluge continued without respite. Then it stopped as suddenly as it had begun, leaving the air cooler. But the storm hadn't passed. The sky was a little lighter overhead but there was no sign of a break in the clouds and the thunder continued to circle around.

While Kathryn mopped up, Charles hauled in the almost waterlogged dinghy and baled it out. Then he tried to discover where they had got to. The shore was nearer now than it had been all day, but on their present course they seemed to be steering away from it. Could they be off the North Foreland already? There was a buoy some

157

distance astern of them, which they must have passed during the rainstorm, but he couldn't identify it. After a little hesitation he put the ship about and ran back to read the name. He was glad he had done so, for it proved to be the Longnose, and that meant a change of course. He swung the boat's head round again, and they began to run down the eastern coast of Thanet.

There was still no breath of wind to stir the sails and by now the tide was turning against them. *Witch*'s speed was soon reduced to a mere knot or two and for hours they seemed to be looking at an unchanging landscape. The bad weather had driven all the holiday-makers off the beaches and the shore had a desolate appearance. The sea was even emptier. There were a few wisps of smoke on the horizon and once or twice a small freighter or a fishing vessel passed them at a distance, but no one took any notice of them.

Just after two o'clock Charles touched Kathryn's arm and pointed away to starboard where a stone jetty girdled a forest of masts. "That must be Ramsgate Harbour," he shouted above the engine noise.

"Keep going!" she called back. "We're all right." She attempted a bar of her sailing theme-song, which had never failed to wring a sardonic smile from Charles in the past—"Where ignorance is bliss . . ." But this time he could manage nothing but a grimace in response.

The afternoon passed slowly and monotonously. They took short, regular turns at the tiller, for the seat in the cockpit was hard and the steering position cramping. Whoever was relieved brewed tea or attended to the minor chores around the boat or rested in the cabin away from the maddening beat of the engine. They were both beginning to feel the strain of the long day, and though Charles still felt twinges of concern for Kathryn's safety he was glad indeed to have her help.

In the early evening a light breeze sprang up from the north-east and the sails, now almost dry, billowed out gracefully once more. With a sigh of thankfulness Charles switched off the engine and a blessed peace descended upon the boat. *Witch* seemed a bit sluggish under her shortened mainsail but the tide was beginning to push her along again and Charles decided to wait a little before making any change.

Before long he was glad he had done so, for the breeze quickly freshened and the seas began to whip up with dramatic suddenness. This, he thought grimly, was what the glass had prophesied. He saw an unbroken wall of slanting rain advancing upon them and took a bearing on a buoy which he thought must be the North-East Goodwin. Then the weather closed down, and seamarks and landmarks alike were blotted out. White-faced and sick, Kathryn was presently forced to retire to the cabin. Charles wrestled with the tiller and struggled to keep on course. If they tried to run for shelter now, they'd probably only pile up ashore. Somehow, they'd got to stick it out.

The rainstorm passed but the wind continued to strengthen and every moment the sea became more confused. *Witch* was plunging and rearing like a restive horse. Astern, the dinghy was careering about wildly, straining and tugging at its painters. In the gusts it was as much as Charles could do to hold the sheet and he realised with dismay that even the reefed sail might be too much for the boat before long. Perhaps he ought to take in another reef at once—or had he already left it too late? The cabin top was wet and treacherous and there was nothing at all to hang on to. Perhaps the lesser risk was to stay where he was. Perhaps the weather would moderate. Perhaps . . .

He could hardly believe that the sea could have gathered such fnry in so short a time. By now it was an amazing spectacle—a tossing wilderness of grey and white, smoking with spume. Savage gusts whipped the foam from the wave tops and filled the air with flying, blinding spray. Water and sky were indistinguishable, and soon he had lost all track of their position. They were somewhere between the Goodwin Sands and the coast, that was all he knew, and probably dangerously near the shore because the wind was blowing them steadily towards it. He steered farther out to sea in an attempt to make up for the leeway, but he no longer felt that he had the situation under control.

So far *Witch* had shipped very little water over the stern but the waves were rolling down on her like hungry animals and sometimes it seemed that the dinghy, towering above the cockpit, would be swept aboard. Charles watched it with growing apprehension as it climbed and plunged and sheered about. Suddenly the end came. There was a loud crack, and two bits of shredded rope hung from the stern. "Tender to *Witch*" had gone, and there was no chance whatever of picking her up.

Kathryn heard the noise and peered anxiously out of the cabin. "What was that?"

"The dinghy's gone."

"Oh." She looked at him blankly. "What shall we do?"

"Just carry on. We could never have used it anyway in a sea like this. We'll think of something."

She nodded. She looked very sick.

The boat suddenly gave a lurch as a fresh blast struck the board-hard sail, and for a moment she lay almost on her beam ends. From the cabin came a succession of slithering crashes and a cry from Kathryn as gear and stores burst adrift. Charles let the sheet run out and braced his feet against the side of the cockpit. They couldn't go on like this! The storm was getting worse, and at this rate he'd soon be exhausted. They ought to be reefed right down—they ought to be carrying storm canvas, or perhaps none at all. Perhaps they'd do better to rely on the engine. With the wind shrieking round his ears it was hard to decide anything. At least there wouldn't be so much leeway under bare poles. . . .

The boat was labouring frightfully, the mast was bending under the weight of the bellying sail. God, this was awful! Grey-faced, he looked across the streaming cabin top. Somehow he'd *got* to get the sail down. He tried to think of the drill. If he turned the boat's head into the wind and held on to the boom . . .

At that moment the problem was settled for him. Another gust came screaming out of the sky and with a report like a cannon the mainsail blew out. Instantly the boat became a wild confusion of flogging canvas, while flying ribbons streamed away to leeward.

He shouted to Kathryn, and as she staggered to the tiller he bent to the engine and cranked it. Miraculously, it started at the first turn and kept going. "Keep her into the wind," he yelled. "I've got to get that sail."

With Kathryn's agonised "*Be careful!*" in his ears he forced himself to climb up on to the heaving cabin roof and scramble forward on his hands and knees to the mast.

The boom had come amidships now that *Witch* was head to wind and he steadied himself against it, winding his legs round the wooden tabernacle while the remnants of the torn sail flailed around his head. He groped blindly for the halyard, cast it off by touch, and gave a savage jerk at the canvas. Suddenly the sail came down with a rush, enveloping him. He fought it as though it were a living monster, subduing it foot by foot. As he got the lashings round it, Kathryn managed to lift the swinging boom into its crutches and furl the slatting foresail with a pull on the cord. Then a big sea lifted the boat's bows and tumbled him, soaked and gasping, into the cockpit.

The immediate crisis was over, but he knew that they were still in mortal danger. Now that the steadying influence of the sail was lost there was nothing to check the wild motion of the boat. The pitching became much worse—every few seconds the stern was lifted clean out of the water and the propeller raced uselessly, so that it was difficult to keep way on her. By now Charles had abandoned all thoughts of holding a course and was content to steer straight into the eye of the wind. Sea room was what they needed; sea room until the gale blew itself out and they could get their bearings again.

He looked at Kathryn's huddled figure and his salt-caked face twisted into a grin. "Some people do this sort of thing for fun!" he shouted.

She tried hard to smile in response. She had been desperately afraid when he had been up on the cabin top. She knew that he wasn't equipped, in strength or knowledge, for the ordeal they were going through. Neither was she. She was frightened. They were both frightened. But if courage meant not letting fear dictate action, theirs wasn't exhausted yet.

As dusk closed down on the heaving water the wind moderated a little, and in spite of everything they began to feel more hopeful. The glass had steadied—perhaps the worst of the storm was over. Even the seas seemed to have lost some of their venom. The waves were still hammering at the hull and breaking over the bows in shattering explosions of foam, but the boat wasn't being flung about quite so much and if she hadn't foundered by now, after all this punishment, there was no reason why she shouldn't stand up to anything—provided the engine kept going. While Kathryn held the tiller, Charles managed to top up the petrol in the tank. About a gallon went into the sea from the jerrycan and in the struggle he lost the funnel overboard, but the tank was full again and the motor was good for another eight or nine hours' running.

Darkness was falling now, and very soon the night was so black that he could barely see Kathryn beside him. He went below and lit the gimballed cabin lamp, but there was no possibility of lighting the navigation lamps. Not that it mattered much—being run down was one of the lesser risks now. He stared out into the featureless night, searching in vain for the guiding flash of a buoy. They must have travelled miles since his doubtful identification of the North-East Goodwin—but in which direction? Again, it hardly mattered—they could do nothing more for the safety of the ship than they were already doing. And they could do nothing more for themselves. They couldn't sleep or rest in this turmoil of movement; neither of them had any desire to eat. All they could do was wait, and endure.

Or was it? Suddenly, from somewhere astern of them, Charles heard a sound that jerked him into action—a sound that rose above the clatter of the engine and the moaning of the wind. Fearfully, he peered into the swirling darkness. It sounded like the crash of breakers. He waited for a moment, gripping Kathryn's arm, and then the thundering roll burst upon his ears again, louder and nearer. It *was* breakers. In that instant he knew that what he had been most afraid of had happened—although the boat's head had been pointing out to sea, the engine hadn't been powerful enough to overcome the pressure of the wind. They were being blown ashore!

Once more he thrust the tiller into Kathryn's hands and rushed forward over the cabin top. There could be no hesitation now—the next thirty-seconds might decide their fate. A sudden plunge almost flung him into the sea but he grabbed the mast just in time and regained his balance and dropped to his knees on the heaving foredeck. He clung there for a moment, waiting for his opportunity, and as the boat steadied itself he heaved up the thirty-pound anchor and hurled it overboard. The chain rattled out fast—fifteen fathoms, twenty fathoms, perhaps more. The breakers were nearer, much nearer—he could make out the line of foam. Then there came a jerk and the rattling stopped—the chain was all out. He hung on to the mast, watching the shore. Nearer?—or not? For a while he wasn't sure. Then he gave an encouraging shout and scrambled back into the cockpit. The anchor was holding!

It had been a near thing, though—in the troughs, their keel must be almost touching the bottom. He tried to consider their plight without panic. The wind *was* dropping —in an hour they might be safe if only they could ride it out. But could they? Every time *Witch* rose on a wave the bows snubbed on the chain with a jolt that shook the ship. If that continued, something was bound to give way. There were things people did in emergencies like this—he seemed to remember Peter saying something about hauling in a bit of the chain and lashing a weight on to it to cushion the shock. But would he be able to haul in the chain against the wind, even with the engine running fully? And where was the weight? Perhaps he'd do better to get the second anchor from the forepeak and have it in readiness. He turned towards the cabin just as the bows rose again. There was a hideous jolt, and suddenly the snubbing ceased.

He knew then that it was too late to do anything. The chain had parted.

Now they were driving straight ashore, and a moment later *Witch* struck with an impact that knocked them off their feet. She was held, shuddering, as the water receded and then a new wave lifted her and she raced forward and struck again. A breaker came roaring over the bows and burst in a blinding sea of foam. The engine spluttered and died As the boat crashed down on the hard sand there was a rending, splintering smash as though a box had been dropped from a height.

Charles yelled to Kathryn to hang on and dived below through boiling surf. The life-jackets were still hanging on their peg. He grabbed them and staggered out. The pounding was incessant and he knew the ship must break up soon. Seas hammered and raged around and above them. Breasting the surging water he jammed one of the jackets over Kathryn's head and fastened the strings with numbed fingers. Then he struggled into the other one.

The breakers were carrying the stricken boat ever closer in. Kathryn suddenly gave a shout of warning as a wave, larger than any yet, towered above them and broke with the force of an avalanche. Charles had just time to grab her wrist before they were swept from the cockpit and carried shorewards on the surging crest.

At that point, thought ended. Water enveloped them, pressing them down, roaring in their ears. Something hit Charles a violent blow in the chest and he had to loose his grip. He kicked out with bursting lungs, hampered by his sea-boots, helped by his jacket. As he broke surface he gulped air and looked frantically about him. Kathryn was still at his side, striking out on her own. A moment later he felt the ground under him and yelled to her to keep going. Another wave broke over them, hurling them flat, battering them against the sand, but when its fury was spent they were nearer their goal. Half-drowned, fighting for life, they still struggled forward side by side. Then they were clawing their way up a pebbly beach, out of reach of the waves. Bits of the boat's gear followed them in.

CHAPTER III

FOR a while they lay gasping on the stones, too exhausted to speak, too battered and bruised to think. Their struggle had been instinctive, their reactions were purely physical. Only as strength returned did their minds begin to function again, and then they knew that they had suffered irreparable disaster. Kathryn threw herself against Charles and burst into uncontrollable weeping.

He gathered her in his arms and held her close, but no words of comfort came to him. As he gazed out through the noisy darkness at the wreck of their hopes, everything seemed at an end. Boat, stores, all gone. No clothes but those they lay and shivered in. No means of escape any more. He clung to her, and cursed the luck that had saved him. It would have been better if he'd been lost in the surf—at least she would have been freed then from this endless nightmare.

Presently her sobs ceased and she sat up, pushing her tangled hair out of her eyes. "I'm sorry, darling," she said. "I just couldn't help it."

"Do you feel better?"

"I'm quite all right now."

"At least I put you ashore!"

"Don't, I can't bear it. . . . Where do you think we are?"

"I've no idea. Somewhere in Kent."

She looked around. "There's a light up on the cliff—there may be a road. Do you think we're far from Dover?"

"I don't know—not very far, perhaps. Does it make any difference?"

"Of course it does. If I could reach Dover I could get my suitcase from the cloakroom and tidy up and then I could go and fetch the car. . . . Charles, we've got to go on trying—we can't give up now."

"How could you get up to town?—you've no money."

She thrust her hand into the pocket of her windcheater. "I have—money and passport and everything. I put it here for safety."

"That certainly helps," he said, but his tone was still apathetic. "Suppose you did manage to get the car—where would we go?"

"Anywhere, for the moment. Back to the cottage. After all, the police aren't on your track—they don't know what's happened to you."

"They'll know in the morning, as soon as the wreck's reported. They'll probably find some of my belongings strewn along the beach and that will settle it."

"They may think you've been drowned."

He sat watching the surf hammering at the pitiful hulk on the beach and suddenly his mood of resignation left him. "By God, Kathryn, I believe you're right—there *may* still be a chance."

"Perhaps a better one than ever," she said eagerly, "because if they do think so they'll stop looking for you. The newspapers will say you're dead and everyone will lose interest."

"They're bound to think it odd when my body isn't washed up, though."

"I don't see why. You might easily have been swept overboard in the storm when you were still a long way out to sea."

"Yes, there's that. I might—very easily!"

"The only thing is, have we left any marks on the beach?"

He peered into the darkness. "I shouldn't think so, not on these pebbles. Anyway, hundreds of people must use these beaches every day."

"Then we should be all right." Kathryn got up. "I think I ought to start now—it must be getting on for midnight and we don't know how far I'll have to go. What about you, darling?—oughtn't we to find a safe place for you to hide?"

"I suppose so. God, how I wish I didn't have to leave everything to you! Still, I can walk with you till daybreak —there can't be many people about now so it should be safe enough."

"We'll have to be careful about car headlights—we must look awfully like survivors." She ran a comb through her hair and tried to squeeze some of the water out of her clothes. "What shall we do with the life-jackets?"

"Take them with us and push them into a ditch, I should think." He gathered them up and stuffed them under his arm. Then they set off slowly along the beach.

By now the wind had dropped to a mere zephyr, but the air was cool and they were both glad to be on the move again. They picked their way cautiously over the pebbles, avoiding any patches of sand until they were well away from the wreck. Presently Kathryn pointed to a gap in the chalky cliff. They scrambled up on to a smooth grassy slope and a moment later they had reached the road.

It was a typical seaside "front", with a wide paved promenade, and flower-beds set in short turf, and pavilions, and a row of huge Victorian hotels on the side away from the sea. Neither of them recognised the place, but whatever it was there was no doubt about the direction they must take. They turned southwards, stepping out quickly to keep warm. Once or twice a car passed them, but the approaching headlights gave them plenty of warning and they dropped to a lovers' stroll until the danger was over. They met no other pedestrians—the holidaymakers had evidently given the day up as a hopeless one and gone to bed.

After a mile or so the promenade ended and the road turned sharply inland. They had no choice but to follow it. Already they were beginning to flag—Charles still wore his sea-boots, which were clumsy and squelched water at every step, and Kathryn's sodden shoes were threatening to raise blisters. They talked little, conserving their strength. Presently they passed through a small village and came out on another road, a much wider one. At the T-junction there was a signpost. One finger, pointing northwards, said "Deal 3". The other said "Dover 5".

Kathryn gave a sigh of thankfulness. She had begun to wonder whether she would ever get to Dover, but five miles wasn't much, even with a blister. The problem now was different—how and where to pass the night. There was no point in arriving in Dover before the station cloakroom opened.

They plodded on at a slower pace. The road was much more rural now, with fields and hedges on both sides. Charles was still hugging the life-jackets, looking for a place to hide them. Suddenly he stopped by a farm gate, pointing to a haystack. "What about pushing them in there?"

They climbed the gate and approached the stack. It was an old one that had been knocked about a bit, and much of the hay was loose. It smelt delicious. Charles stuffed the jackets deep into the heart of the stack and then looked thoughtfully around. There was no sign of any farmhouse. "Why shouldn't we stay here?" he said. "We can keep warm in the hay and let our clothes dry and it's a good spot for you to leave me in tomorrow. I shan't find a better hiding place."

She agreed at once. Now that he'd suggested it, she knew that she couldn't walk another step.

Silently they stripped off their clothes and spread them out on the side of the stack away from the road. Then they crept naked into the hay. It was prickly and uncomfortable at first, but as they bedded down and ceased to move the discomfort passed. In a little while they were warm and cosy, and presently they slept.

Just before daybreak Charles stirred, and the movement roused Kathryn. She was fully awake on the instant, alarmed in case she had overslept. She pushed the hay aside and looked out at the pale sky.

"I must go," she said, "it'll soon be light." She wriggled out of her cocoon and dressed quickly. Her clothes were still damp and sticky from the salt water and she shivered a little as she put them on, but she felt immensely refreshed by the night's rest.

"I wish I could come with you," Charles said wistfully, watching her struggle into her shoes. "How's the blister?"

"Better. Everything's much better." She brushed bits of hay from her windcheater and tidied herself up as well as she could. "How do I look? Still like a survivor?"

"You'll get by."

"I hope so. Now let's see—suppose there's a train to London between eight and nine. Say ten-thirty at the flat—half an hour there—two hours to drive back. I should be here with the car soon after one."

"I'll be counting the minutes—but don't break your neck. And watch out for police—they may have begun to take an interest in you again by now."

"I'll be very careful. You too! Don't show yourself, will you?"

"You needn't worry about that. I'll lie doggo."

"I'll bring some food back with me."

He kissed her, and smiled. "I was going to say I don't know what I'd do without you, but I know only too well! Good-bye, darling. Good luck!"

When she had gone he returned to his burrow and lay there quietly, thinking about his prospects. He still thought that Kathryn was probably right about the wreck—the police would almost certainly conclude that he'd been drowned in the storm. Considering how unsuccessful their hunt had been, they would be only too glad to announce such a satisfactory end. One thing worried him a little—the possibility that Kathryn might have been seen aboard *Witch* from the bridge of some passing steamer. Nothing had come very close, but someone might have used glasses before the weather shut down and if it were reported that a woman had been aboard the boat the police would assume it was Kathryn and they'd be after her for the whole story. That would mean more invention—she'd have to say that he had been drowned and that she had struggled ashore alone and her activities afterwards would be difficult to account for. . . . He wished he'd thought to discuss all that with her. Still, she'd been in the cabin a good deal and the chances were that she wouldn't have been seen.

If the police *did* write him off as dead, everything would be changed. He could let his beard grow, and get some rimmed spectacles with plain glass instead of lenses, and take a new name—it shouldn't be impossible to start a new life. Of course, it would be only a stop-gap existence—there'd be no future in it for him, and even less for Kathryn—but it would give them a breathing space while they searched for new evidence and perhaps something would turn up in the end. It would certainly be a lot better than being on the run.

He looked out, and saw that it was almost daylight. He'd better get his clothes, or someone might notice them. He crawled out of his hole and dressed, and then he pulled

169

some of the loose hay over him and lay watching the sun come up. It was going to be a fine day—the sort of day they should have had yesterday! He felt ravenously hungry, but he could see nothing fit to eat. The field was pasture, the blackberries in the hedge were still green. In any case, it was safer not to show himself, even for a moment. He chewed the end of a straw and thought how hungry Kathryn must be, too, and about the blister on her heel.

The hours passed uneventfully. There was more activity on the road as labourers cycled to work and pedestrians strolled by, chatting, and the coastal traffic swelled, but Charles felt well screened by the stack. As the sun grew warmer he basked gratefully in its heat, sticking his head and shoulders out and keeping a watchful eye on the gate.

Suddenly he heard something that stirred unpleasant memories—the barking of a dog not far away. He turned quickly in the direction of the noise and saw to his horror that a small boy was coming across the field towards him with a snapping terrier at his heels. They were having a game together, the boy throwing sticks and the dog recovering them. Though their progress was desultory they were clearly making for the gate.

Charles hesitated for a moment—then dived into the burrow where he had spent the night, pulling the hay down over the opening and lying motionless, hardly daring to breathe. The yapping came nearer—receded—came nearer still. A moment later the dog was snuffling at the opening and the boy was shouting encouragement—"Go on, Spot! —get a rabbit!" Charles drew farther back into the hay but the terrier was growing more and more excited. In desperation he stuck his head out and tried to shoo it away, ferocious in face and gesture but not daring to shout. The animal continued to bark and leap, its short tail wagging with pleasure at the size of its quarry. Just then the boy came running up to join in the hunt. He caught sight of Charles's head and stopped in his tracks, staring.

"Hallo!" he said, keeping his distance. He was wearing a tee-shirt and shorts and looked about ten years old.

"Hallo!" said Charles, emerging from the stack with what dignity he could manage.

The boy came a cautious step nearer. He had a fresh, intelligent face, and freckles. "Are you a tramp?"

"A sort of tramp," said Charles.

"You don't talk like a tramp."

"I'm on a walking tour."

The boy gazed at his crumpled, salt-stained clothes. "You're all wet!"

"Yes, I got caught in the rain—that's why I slept in the stack."

"You've made an awful mess of my dad's hay."

Charles tried to smile. "I'll tidy it up before I go."

The boy continued to stare at him. "I think I've seen you before, mister."

"I shouldn't think so," said Charles, fear tugging at his heart. He began moving towards the gate. At all costs he must get away from this chattering menace.

"I have, though," said the youth, pursuing him triumphantly, "and I know *where*. I saw your picture in the Sunday paper. A big picture . . .!"

Charles stopped edging away. Only action could save him now. If the boy went home and talked it wouldn't be long before the hunt started again—and this time they'd find him. Find him, and hang him!—just when freedom seemed in sight. He took a step forward and grabbed a slim wrist. "Now listen to me . . ." he said, roughly.

A look of terror leapt into the child's eyes, and with a feeling of hot shame Charles let the wrist go. If his neck depended on it, he couldn't bully the lad. He stood for a despairing moment, watching boy and dog scampering away across the field. Then he turned and climbed the gate into the road.

For Kathryn, all had gone smoothly. It took her an hour and a half to walk into Dover and by the time she reached the station her clothes were quite dry. She retrieved her suitcase, gave herself as good a grooming as possible, and twenty minutes later caught a train to town. She did a bit of shopping on her way to the flat, made a flask of coffee there, collected the car, and by eleven was driving out of London again, just as she had planned. The journey passed without incident and at ten minutes to one she parked the car opposite the haystack.

Keeping a careful look-out for approaching traffic she leaned over the gate and softly called Charles's name.

When she got no response she thought he must be sleeping and went in to rouse him. She poked about in the hay, gazed across the field, anxiously scanned the hedgerow. He seemed to have disappeared without trace.

Mystified and deeply worried, she returned to the road. She couldn't begin to imagine what had happened. It was incredible that he should willingly have left the place in daylight, knowing the risk. It seemed equally unlikely that anyone could have found him here. Even if he'd slept, he'd have been quite safe deep in the hay unless someone had disturbed the stack—and there was absolutely no sign of that. And if he'd been awake, he'd have been certain to notice anyone coming.

Perhaps that was the explanation. Perhaps he'd seen someone approaching and decided to move to some other field. In that case, he couldn't be far away. She gave a couple of loud toots on the car horn and waited hopefully, but after five minutes he still hadn't appeared. Of course, he might have had to go some distance to find another stack, and if so he wouldn't want to risk the journey back. He might be waiting for her to seek him out.

She got back into the car and drove slowly along the road for about a mile, stopping at every gate and hooting loudly. When that produced no result she repeated the process in the other direction. After that, she hardly knew what to do. They'd made no plans to cover this sort of situation. Searching any further was hopeless, for she had no idea where to look.

She returned to the gate and parked the car on the grass verge and smoked a cigarette. By now she was really frightened. She tried to put herself in his position, to think of some convincing reason why he should have gone, but no theory seemed to meet the case. Utterly baffled, she continued to wait.

Three o'clock came, and four o'clock, and still there was no sign of him. Suddenly, in her agitation, a dreadful idea occurred to her—he might have been taken ill! It was true he'd seemed all right when she'd left him, but perhaps the long strain of the hunt and the exposure and the shock of that awful wreck had been too much for him—perhaps he'd wandered off without knowing what he was doing. If so, the only hope was to scour the whole district, cover every road. Desperately, she got out her map and planned a route.

During the next two hours she travelled nearly forty miles, along main roads and side roads and mere lanes. With every mile the task appeared more hopeless, the whole business more inexplicable. She would never find him this way. She felt completely worn out, absolutely beaten. Yet it was unthinkable that she should give up, and just drive away.

She cruised slowly through the main streets of Deal, thinking that perhaps she ought to go back to the haystack, which was still their only rendezvous. Traffic lights ahead of her changed to red and she stopped by the kerb, mechanically examining the faces of the passers-by. There was a man selling newspapers on the corner, and as he held one out to a customer a headline caught her eye. A huge headline.

HILARY RECAPTURED

CHAPTER IV

THAT night, after a brief telephone call, Kathryn drove to Surbiton to see Charles's solicitor. She would have preferred to get her information from Murgatroyd in this final crisis, but it appeared that he was out of the country. The rather aloof lawyer would have to do.

Robert Fairey's manner, as he shook hands with her, was formal. The hour was very late, he had had an exacting day at the office, and he knew there was nothing whatever that he or anyone else could do for Hilary. This visit was pointless, and he feared an hysterical scene. But Kathryn had by now recovered from the first brutal impact of the news and she had herself well in hand. She needed reassurance only on one point.

"Mr. Fairey, have you found out when the execution will be?"

For one awful moment she thought his lips were framing the word "tomorrow". Then he said, "Tuesday, I understand. Five days from now."

She gave a little sigh and sat down. Five days!

"Would you please tell me," she said, "the names of the hotels where Louise Hilary stayed?"

He glanced at her in surprise. "Why, yes, I can do that if you wish. The one she spent most time at was the Superbe at Brighton. The other was the Regina-Grand at Bournemouth."

"Are they the only ones?"

"They are the only ones we know about."

"Mr. Fairey, exactly what inquiries did you have made at these places? Who went to them?"

He hesitated, and for a moment she thought he would refuse to answer. Then, as though he had decided that there could be no harm in humouring her now, he said, "A man named Hawkins and a woman named Rouse.

174

They were both very experienced private inquiry agents whom I had used on many previous occasions."

"What instructions were they given?"

"They were told to look for evidence that Louise Hilary had met some man at these hotels. As you know, they didn't find any."

"Do you know how they went to work?"

Fairey flushed under the catechism. "That I can't say, but I have no doubt they were as thorough as circumstances permitted."

"I don't suppose the hotels were very co-operative?"

"One could hardly expect them to be, but these people are used to working by devious means. They would certainly have looked at the registers and questioned the staffs."

"All the same, the truth may have escaped them?"

"It may, Miss Forrester, but there is no reason why we should suppose so. After all, those inquiries were little more than a shot in the dark. There was never any real indication that Mrs. Hilary wasn't alone on these occasions."

"She took good care there shouldn't be."

"That was the theory we were working on, of course. The fact remains that no one ever accompanied her to these places, no one registered with her, no one was ever seen associating with her, and she paid her own bills. What's more, she was always alone in her room when the chamber-maid went in in the mornings."

"She could easily have been discreet by day and hos-pitable by night. The man could have had a separate room, and visited her when the hotel was quiet."

"All I can say," Fairey repeated patiently, "is that no evidence was found to support such a theory."

Kathryn got up. "Well, thank you for the information you've given me. I'm sorry I had to worry you so late at night, but I couldn't wait until the morning."

"Please don't disturb yourself on that account." He looked at her curiously. "May I ask what you intend to do?"

"I'm going to try to find that evidence."

"At this stage? I'm afraid you're wasting your time."

"Time, Mr. Fairey, is something I'm going to have a great deal of after Tuesday. Good-bye."

"Good-bye," he said. He stood watching her from the door for a moment. Then he gave a little shrug and went inside. Feverish activity, however futile, was no doubt better than hysteria.

The reception clerk at the Superbe showed by a quick flicker of interest that he recognised Kathryn when she presented herself next morning at the hotel. She feared for a moment that he might say the place was full or raise some objection to her staying, but he gave her the book to sign and handed her key to the porter without comment. The first hurdle was passed.

She soon discovered, though, that making inquiries was going to be more difficult than she had imagined. Her belief that she might do better than Fairey's detectives had been based on her old success as a reporter and interviewer, but now it became apparent that mere technique was not enough. It was one thing to ask questions when you were an unknown newspaperwoman or a popular celebrity and quite another when you were the notorious mistress of a man who was about to be hanged for murder. Wherever she went she sensed an atmosphere and knew she was the cynosure of disapproving eyes, the single subject of hotel gossip. It wasn't surprising, of course, for to the uninformed her appearance in a public place at such a time must seem, to put it mildly, the height of bad taste. In the dining-room, women glared and men stared; in the lounge bar, voices were lowered as she entered. Whether from embarrassment, or a healthy regard for their own interests, the staff shied away from her the moment they had attended to her legitimate requirements. The prospects couldn't have been bleaker.

She still hoped that with patience and the exercise of great discretion she might be able to bribe or wheedle her way into someone's confidence, but by the end of the second day she knew that the hope wasn't going to be realised. She had had a few words with the boy who washed the cars in the garage, with the young barman when there were no other customers present, and with her own chambermaid in the privacy of her room, but that was all. And none of them had been able to give her any helpful information.

On the second night, however, she did succeed in uncovering one small but suggestive fact. The Irish maid who came to turn down her bed in the evening remembered Louise well and seemed quite prepared to talk about her. The reason soon emerged—Louise, it appeared, had reported her for "insolence" and she had nearly lost her job in consequence. The suggestive fact was that Louise had always occupied a room on the very top floor, because she found it less noisy there. Slight though the clue was, Kathryn felt confirmed in her suspicions. What she needed to know now was whether any *man* had consistently preferred a room on the quiet top floor, but about that the Irish girl couldn't help her.

By next day, the atmosphere in the hotel had grown still more hostile. The reception clerk, who had begun by being friendly enough in a reserved sort of way, was now very distant in his manner. The bluff, old-school-tie manager, passing her in one of the corridors, gave her a stony glance. If she were going to look at the hotel register, she decided, she must do it quickly while she still had the opportunity.

The large, heavily bound volume was kept permanently on the reception desk and presumably anyone could go and look at it. Even *she* might be permitted a hasty glance. But that wouldn't be enough—she needed to study it—to spend time with it. A formal request would certainly be refused. In the circumstances, direct action seemed the only course.

Shortly before dinner, when most of the guests were dressing, or drinking in the bar, and the rush of new arrivals was over, she took up a position near the hotel entrance, as though she were waiting for someone. The hall porter was temporarily absent from the foyer; the reception clerk was busy with his books.

Her chance soon came. After a few moments a buzzer sounded beside the clerk's desk and he went into the manager's office. Kathryn gave a quick glance round, walked across to the counter, swept up the register, and without a pause carried it upstairs to her room. There she turned the key in the lock and settled down to examine its pages.

At once, she found herself up against insuperable

obstacles. The hotel was a large and busy one, and every day brought many new registrations. She turned to the page where Louise had last signed her name, on a Saturday back in May, and counted thirty-three other arrivals on that day. Of these, no fewer than eleven were unaccompanied males, and four more, who had signed with initials instead of Christian names, seemed more likely to be men than women. Nor was the mere number the only problem, for many of the addresses were incomplete. "Arthur Jones, London" was a typical entry. Moreover, quite apart from the difficulty of tracing a person without an address, there was no reason to suppose that if some man had made a rendezvous here with Louise he had necessarily registered under his own name. It was much more likely that he would have given a fictitious one. And there was the added complication that a woman like Louise might have met different men on different occasions.

For a while Kathryn stared helplessly at the book. Then she suddenly had an idea. If by any chance the same man *had* been here on more than one occasion, he must surely have registered under the same name each time, otherwise someone might have noticed the change. Having once chosen his alias, he'd have had to stick to it.

Laboriously, but with a specific purpose now, she worked through the record. Louise, she found, had entered her signature on five separate occasions over a period of about eight months. On sheets of hotel paper she made five lists of unaccompanied men who had registered around those periods. Then she went carefully through the lists, checking them one against the other. Almost at once she found what she had hoped for. On two occasions a "Stephen Lauterbach" of "Hampstead" had signed the book on the same day as Louise. The signature was a careless scrawl.

She had little doubt now that she was on the right track. It was a sickening thought that she might have made the discovery weeks ago if she hadn't been ill, but she couldn't blame herself for that—and she couldn't really blame Fairey's agents, either. It had taken her more than an hour to isolate this crucial fact, and she could well understand how the detectives had missed it. They, after all, hadn't been personally involved to the extent of not caring what happened to them—they couldn't have been expected to carry off the register. They'd have had to content themselves with a quick glance through the book and that would have told them nothing.

She sat back and considered the next step. The first thing, obviously, was to restore the register to its place before its loss was discovered. After that, there were half a dozen questions she was eager to have answered, and now that she had something definite to go on perhaps she'd be able to persuade the management to talk. Which room had "Stephen Lauterbach" had?—there was no indication in the book, but the information was sure to be on record in the office. Had he reserved his room by phone or letter? Had he said anything about the top floor? Which chambermaid had looked after him? What was he like in appearance? Had he paid his bill by cheque or in cash? Hopeful lines of inquiry opened out in all directions.

She shut the register and put the sheets of paper in her handbag. She was about to leave the room when she heard raised voices in the corridor and a moment later there came a sharp double knock at her door.

It was too late!—they'd already missed the book.

For a second she wondered if she should try to bluff it out, pretend she hadn't seen the thing, but she decided there was no point. The reception clerk had probably noticed her hanging about in the hall—and, anyway, who else would have taken it? A bold front seemed best. Assuming as calm an expression as possible, she opened the door. The manager and the reception clerk were both there.

The manager's frown was forbidding. "Miss Forrester, the hotel register has been removed. Do you know anything about it?"

"Yes," she said, "I took it. I'm sorry, but there was something I simply had to find out. You had a man named Lauterbach staying here . . ."

The reception clerk stepped into the room and gathered up the register. The manager said icily, "I must ask you to leave at once."

"*Please!* I need your help so badly. If you'll only let me explain. . . ."

"Madam, unless you are out of this building within half an hour I shall call the police and have you ejected. Your behaviour has been grossly improper. That's all I have to say."

Red-faced, he snatched the register from the clerk and marched indignantly away.

Kathryn moved that night to another hotel and first thing in the morning she drove on to the Regina-Grand at Bournemouth, which, in spite of its name, proved to be a more modest establishment than the Superbe. This time her approach was different. At Brighton, with a stay of several days in front of her, it had seemed hopeless to try to conceal her identity, but she had no intention of stopping at this place and she had bought a pair of sun-glasses which would at least prevent her from being recognised the moment she entered the door.

At the desk, she launched into a complicated story about a friend of hers having stayed at the hotel about a week ago and left some books for her to collect. While the receptionist, an amiable young girl, made inquiries, Kathryn found the page in the register where Louise Hilary had signed her name and quickly ran her eye down the list of unattached males. There was no "Stephen Lauterbach" of "Hampstead", but there was another signature that she found almost as interesting—that of a "Paul Liefschitz" of "London". It seemed to her that the handwriting in both cases was rather similar.

The best thing now, she decided, was to put her cards on the table while she was still in good odour at the hotel. Thanking the receptionist, and agreeing that she must have come to the wrong place, she asked if she might have a private word with the manager. He turned out to be a younger and friendlier man than his counterpart at the Superbe, but when she told him who she was and why she was there his expression became very serious. He listened to what she had to say about "Stephen Lauterbach" and "Paul Liefschitz", but told her frankly that it would be as much as his job was worth to discuss the hotel's guests with her. She did her best to talk him round, but without success.

At that point, she realised that she had reached a dead end. She was altogether too well known, too mixed up in the case, too unwelcome at any hotel where Louise had stayed, to be able to get any further with her quest on her own. The time had come when she must enlist help.

At eleven o'clock the next morning she drove into Surrey to see Sir John Fawcett by appointment. This time she was shown into the library, and almost at once he joined her.

"My dear Miss Forrester," he said, warmly extending his hand. With concern he saw how tired she looked. "Do sit down! Can I get you anything—a glass of sherry, perhaps?"

She shook her head. "Sir John, I've come to you because I'm quite desperate and you're the only person who can possibly help me."

His shrewd eyes dwelt on her kindly. "Tell me what you think I can do."

"It's about Charles Hilary."

"I imagined it was probably that."

"Do you know about the case—the details, I mean?"

"Indeed I do. I think I've read everything that's been published about it. A most distressing affair."

"Sir John, he didn't do it—they're going to hang an innocent man."

Fawcett gave a slight nod, of understanding rather than of acquiescence. "It's very natural you should think so."

"Oh, I don't expect you to believe it just because I say so, but I think I may be able to prove it. I've been making inquiries and I've found out a lot of new things in the past three days. There *is* another man in the case."

"If you've evidence of that, Miss Forrester, your best course is undoubtedly to go and see Hilary's legal advisers without delay. They are the people to handle new facts."

"Mr. Murgatroyd's in America," said Kathryn, "and the solicitor doesn't take me seriously. Besides, he couldn't do anything. No one can do anything now except the police, and that's why I've come to you."

Fawcett looked taken aback. "I'm not the police, you know. I'm an ordinary citizen, now."

"But you have access to them, Sir John, and you have so much experience. . . . At least, may I tell you about it?"

"You may do that, of course, if you wish."

Kathryn plunged at once into her story. She told about her investigations at the hotels, and about the two visits of

Stephen Lauterbach to the Superbe, and about the similarity of the Bournemouth signature, and about Louise's predilection for top floors. Fawcett listened attentively.

"Well, it's intriguing," he said at last. "Intriguing, but"—he shook his head—"hardly more than that. The fact that this chap Lauterbach's two visits occurred at the same time as Mrs. Hilary's could so easily be a coincidence."

"Not if he turned out to be Paul Liefschitz as well."

"That would certainly make a difference—but then you say yourself you're not absolutely sure about those signatures."

"I'm not sure because I haven't had a chance to compare them properly and I'm not likely to have because if I go back to the Superbe they'll only throw me out again. The whole trouble is that I haven't any standing—it needs someone who can insist on having questions answered and documents produced and only the police can do that. It would be so easy for them. They could photograph the pages of the registers and get experts to examine the writing and they'd soon know whether Lauterbach and Liefschitz were the same man."

"Suppose they were—what would you expect the police to do then?"

"Why, find him, of course. I've been thinking about that and I don't believe it would be difficult. For one thing, he'd hardly have chosen a foreign name every time unless he were a foreigner himself—he probably did it because he speaks with an accent and knew he couldn't get away with 'Smith'. He may even be a registered alien. In any case, everyone at the hotel would be bound to remember him and the police could easily get a complete description. He may have had a car, too, and that would be another way to trace him. I'm absolutely certain they could find him if they tried."

"Oh, I don't doubt they could find him," Fawcett agreed. "The trouble is, they'd have nothing against him. Even if you're right in thinking that he knew Louise Hilary, the fact that he may have been carrying on a clandestine hotel relationship with her doesn't mean that he killed her."

"No, I realise that must seem a big jump, but once the police found him they'd probably get the evidence. There'd be his appearance—if he were the real murderer he'd more or less answer to the description Mrs. Scott gave. She might realise her mistake when she saw him. In any case, he wouldn't have an alibi for the time of the murder."

Fawcett sighed. "Believe me, Miss Forrester, I understand only too well how you must feel, but now that you've come to me I feel bound to speak frankly. The police, I'm sure, wouldn't feel justified in taking any fresh steps on the basis of what is, after all, a mere hypothesis. They have a great deal on their hands, and it isn't part of their job to make defence inquiries."

"Surely it's a part of their job to see that justice is done?"

"They think justice *has* been done. You've got to remember that they're absolutely satisfied with the case they brought against Hilary. If they were starting the investigation all over again from the beginning they might be interested in this man Lauterbach, but as things are they've no reason to be. They're quite sure they arrested the right man and the jury agreed with them. From their point of view, the matter's at an end."

Kathryn looked at him blankly. She had felt so confident she could get the police to help her—if they wouldn't, she scarcely knew where to turn.

"At least there must be *something* I can do," she said.

"It would be no kindness if I encouraged you to think so. It's so very late—in my opinion nothing can affect the outcome now. Even if the whole police force were mobilised to work on these discoveries of yours, any results would be too late to save Hilary."

"Couldn't the Home Secretary postpone the execution while inquiries were being made . . . ?"

"He would do that only if there were new evidence of a most dramatic and irrefutable kind. If I thought there were the least hope I wouldn't hesitate to approach him myself, but I'm afraid there isn't. . . ." He looked at her drawn, despairing face with deep pity. "I hardly know what to say to you. It's not for me to intrude into your feelings, but if you could . . . well, if you could try to reconcile yourself a little . . ."

She picked up her things. "I don't suppose you'll ever know," she said, "what it feels like to have someone you love *almost* safe, but not quite. Good-bye, Sir John, and thank you for listening to me."

"I only wish I could have been of some help." He stood still for a moment, gazing out of the window with a troubled frown. Then he said: "I'll do this, Miss Forrester—I'll ring up the Commissioner straight away and tell him everything you've told me. He'll think I'm off my head, but I'll do it. Don't imagine that he'll take any action, though. He won't."

"You're very kind, Sir John. I'm grateful for that."

"And if there's anything I can do for you personally, at any time, you've only to command me. Good-bye, my dear." In silence he saw her to her car.

CHAPTER V

IT was the evening before the execution. Kathryn was moving slowly along the Chelsea Embankment, without purpose, her eyes downcast and brooding. Her efforts had come to nothing and she had reached the limit of her mental and physical resources. She no longer felt capable of any sharp emotion—her mind was numb. She had been walking since early morning and her feet were as leaden as her brain. She felt so tired that she wished she could die.

She had walked because it had seemed the only thing to do. She couldn't stay still, waiting—she had to keep moving. She had purposely avoided spending these last hours with anyone she knew—she didn't want to talk or to listen. She had crept away, like an animal with a mortal wound.

As she drifted through the Embankment Gardens, past the King's Head where she and Charles had often lingered over a beer, she felt such a wave of weakness come over her that she had to sit down on a seat and rest. She couldn't remember when she had last eaten—all she knew was that food would choke her. She thought of going into the pub and getting herself some brandy, but the effort seemed too great.

She looked at her watch. Seven o'clock. Thirteen hours more.

Behind her, through the shrubbery, she heard laughter. People were sitting on the low stone wall opposite the pub, chatting happily in the evening sun, their tankards beside them. Snatches of conversation reached her—a girl enthusing about fashions, a young man discussing Kon-Tiki, two "hearties" reminiscing about some golf course where there was a particularly tricky bunker on the ninth.

If I don't get that brandy, she thought, I shall pass out. But if I get up I shall probably pass out anyway. Why did

I let myself get into this state? Why didn't I take twenty aspirins, or something, and go to bed and wake up when it was all over?

The air of cheerfulness around her made everything worse. It was these people who were sending Charles to be hanged, yet they seemed unaware of what they were doing. Didn't anyone ever think of the man in the condemned cell, and the people who loved him? She couldn't bear it. She would rest a moment longer, and then go.

The hearty voices were still rattling on . . .

"That fellow Mansad's an amazing chap—the Indians certainly do turn them out. I saw him at Lords in the last Test—absolutely brilliant."

"Yes, I'm sorry I missed that. He wasn't in nearly such good form at the Oval. . . ."

Kathryn stirred. What was that he'd said?

"I can never seem to get down there—the ground's so out of the way for me."

"For me, too. I didn't go—I watched it on TV. Darned sight more comfortable, and you can see everything in close-up."

"You may be right, but I think I'd miss the excitement of the crowd."

"There wasn't much excitement that day, believe me. When I started to look in, the scoreboard showed a hundred and four for four, and when the fifth wicket fell an hour and a half later, they'd only added thirty. Imagine! —thirty runs in ninety minutes! It was deadly . . ."

Kathryn's wooden features came suddenly to life as the spark of a single word touched off a train of memory. Scoreboard? What was it Charles had said about a scoreboard? A strange, confused pattern began to form in her mind, a jostling and crowding of recollections and experiences. Charles despondent in her flat after seeing Louise —a darkened room—the prowess of Little Mo—people . . . And a phrase—"thirty runs in ninety minutes." Ninety minutes for thirty runs. Ninety minutes. She could almost hear them ticking away.

A moment later she had sprung to her feet, no longer aware of fatigue. It was a chance in a thousand, but it was still a chance. God, why hadn't she thought of it before? *She*, of all people?

A taxi crept towards her along the Embankment and she ran forward, signalling wildly.

The commissionaire glanced up sharply as a small figure flashed past his box. "Half a minute, miss . . .!" he called. Then he recognised Kathryn, but before he could speak again she had disappeared from sight and he heard the lift door clang behind her.

Breathlessly she raced through the familiar corridors to the Film Library. Bob Sanderson was sitting with his long legs up on the table, just as he had been that day when she'd come from the interview with Fawcett.

"Kathryn!" he exclaimed, starting to his feet and staring at her as though she were an apparition. Like everyone else in the building, he had been thinking about her on and off all day. "What on earth . . .?"

"Bob," she burst out, "have you got any pictures of the last Test Match at the Oval?"

"Why, yes, I expect so," he said slowly, his eyes still fixed on her. He saw her sway a little, and took her arm. "Here, have a chair—you look all in."

"I'm all right. Hurry, Bob—everything you've got."

"What is it you're after?"

"A face—Charles Hilary's face."

His low whistle, his sudden look of comprehension, told her there was no need to explain anything more. He knew as much about the case as she did. He was off on the instant, rummaging in the shelves, and in a few moments he returned with two flat tins. "Here's the newsreel," he said, "and here's the stuff it was cut from. I'll give you the newsreel first."

She turned to face the screen and he fixed the film in the projector and dimmed the lights. There was a burst of introductory music, the smooth voice of the newsreel commentator, and then a picture of players coming out of the Oval pavilion, with spectators smiling and applauding in the stands.

The scene changed. Close-up of a batsman now. Of a fieldsman running. Of a bowler in action. More people in the distance, with indistinguishable faces. Another stroke, and the ball followed to the boundary. Spectators again, still blurred. A smart catch behind the wicket. A few highlights packed into a minute's film time. Then the newsreel ended, and the screen went white.

"Nothing there," said Kathryn dully.

"There's a lot more yet. Here we go with the rest of it."

The projector whirred again. Kathryn clutched the arms of her chair with clammy hands. A different batsman this time, a different bowler. More strokes, more running. The umpire in his white coat. A ball delivered and a stump flung into the air. A ripple of excitement now, as the batsman walked away from the wicket. And then— what she had been waiting for, praying for! A close-up of the scoreboard that filled the whole screen, just as the Wimbledon indicator had done when she'd sat here before.

"Bob!—stop!"

The picture became a "still". Just below the bottom edge of the scoreboard there was a row of heads and faces— smiling faces, vacuous faces, perspiring faces, all unaware of the telescopic lens upon them. But none of them was Charles.

Kathryn sat back with a little moaning sigh. Perhaps this part of the match had been played before he arrived— or perhaps he'd never actually moved into the camera's eye. He might be the man whose shoulder was just visible beside one of the posts!

"Go on," she said faintly.

Once again the cameras were turned on new men. There was a dreary stretch of play. Thousands must have watched it with boredom, but to Kathryn every second was charged with tension. There wasn't much time left now. The film was becoming scrappy, with short runs lasting only a few moments. These were the bits and pieces. Her nerves screamed. Surely something must happen soon—something to make the camera swing to the board again. She couldn't *stand* it . . .!

The tempo quickened. A fieldsman was running, his hands outstretched. The ball was held—another batsman was marching away. Then the scoreboard filled the screen again, still with its fringe of bobbing heads. The blood pounded behind Kathryn's eyes and everything became misty.

"Bob!—*focus* it!"

His voice came from far away. "It *is* focused, Kathryn."

The screen was swimming and she slumped back in her seat. She was dimly aware of Bob helping her, forcing her head between her knees. The faintness passed. She struggled up and opened her eyes, compelling herself to look.

There, in front of her, was Charles—grim-faced, slightly at an angle, but unmistakably himself.

For a moment she gazed incredulously at the picture. Then she gave a cry. "We've done it, Bob!—we've *done* it! It's him!" She was on her feet, rushing towards the screen, towards the familiar face. But, it wasn't the face she was looking at any more. It was the scoreboard—the scoreboard that could show thirty runs in ninety minutes and that told the time as plainly as a clock if you knew how to read it.

"Bob," she said tensely, "tell me what the figures mean."

He was almost as excited as she was and his hand shook as he pointed. "These show who the bowlers are and these the batsmen—the spectators have cards with names and numbers on, so they can identify the players from the board. These are the total runs—these are the runs made by the last batsman."

"The one who's just got out?"

"That's right—number 5."

"Bob!—we've got to find out *when* he got out."

"That shouldn't be difficult. It was probably mentioned in some report the next day—it often is. Hang on a minute."

She heard him go to a telephone and dial a number. She stood close to the picture, close to Charles. If only the clock would tell the right time!

"Hallo?—is that the *Daily Record*?" Bob's voice shot from bass to treble in his eagerness. "Sports Department please."

He waited. Kathryn waited. The room seemed very close.

"Hallo—is that you, Les? This is Bob. Listen, old boy, I've got a question for you—it's a matter of life and death . . ."

Another interminable wait after he'd explained it all! Kathryn's thoughts were plunging ahead. How long would it take a man to get from the Oval to Kensington? From the scoreboard to Clandon Mews? Five minutes to get through the crowd and out of the ground; several minutes to reach a parked car or descend to the Underground; at least twenty minutes *en route* by car or train, perhaps longer. Say half an hour as a minimum. And Louise had been killed between three-fifteen and three-forty-five, so if Charles had been at the Oval anywhere between those times . . .

She stood like a statue as Bob pressed the receiver to his ear again. "Yes, Les . . .? No, I shouldn't think it matters to a minute or two . . . *The Times?*—well, that's fairly reliable . . . Just *after* . . .? Yes, I see . . . Okay, Les, thanks a lot . . . I'll tell you tomorrow. 'Bye!"

He hung up and turned to Kathryn. "Number 5 was out just after half-past three."

The tears were suddenly flowing unchecked down her cheeks. Without a word she threw her arms round the young man's neck and hugged him. Then she groped for the telephone and asked the operator to get her Sir John Fawcett's number.